SPECIA~~~~~~~~~~~~~~~~~~DERS

THE UL~~~~~~~~~~~~~~~~~~~~~~~~~)N
(registere~~~~~~~~~~~~~~~~~~~~~~~73)
was establi~~~~~~~~~~~~~~~~~~~~~~~for
research, dia~~~~~~~~~~~~~~~~~~~~~~eases.
Exampl~~~~~~~~~~~~~~
the l~~~~~~~

- The Children's Eye Unit at Moorfields Eye Hospital, London
- The Ulverscroft Children's Eye Unit at Great Ormond Street Hospital for Sick Children
- Funding research into eye diseases and treatment at the Department of Ophthalmology, University of Leicester
- The Ulverscroft Vision Research Group, Institute of Child Health
- Twin operating theatres at the Western Ophthalmic Hospital, London
- The Chair of Ophthalmology at the Royal Australian College of Ophthalmologists

You can help further the work of the Foundation by making a donation or leaving a legacy. Every contribution is gratefully received. If you would like to help support the Foundation or require further information, please contact:

THE ULVERSCROFT FOUNDATION
The Green, Bradgate Road, Anstey
Leicester LE7 7FU, England
Tel: (0116) 236 4325

website: www.foundation.ulverscroft.com

LADY ELEANOR'S SECRET

Lady Eleanor feels destined forever to endure the misery of living as an unpaid governess to her brother Edward's children — until she meets Alexander, Lord Bentley. Alex is seeking a suitable wife to care for his children, leaving him to live freely. Then, mistakenly believing he's compromised Eleanor, he makes her an offer, and she accepts with delight. However, on discovering his real motive, Eleanor is horrified. If she tells him the truth he will surely send her away. And while Edward, needing his sister's inheritance, plans to separate them, will Eleanor's secret also ruin everything when it is revealed?

Books by Fenella Jane Miller
Published by The House of Ulverscroft:

FENELLA-JANE MILLER

LADY ELEANOR'S SECRET

Complete and Unabridged

ULVERSCROFT
Leicester

First published in Great Britain in 2011

First Large Print Edition
published 2013

The moral right of the author has been asserted

British Library CIP Data

Miller, Fenella-Jane.
  Lady Eleanor's secret.
  1. Love stories.
  2. Large type books.
  I. Title
  823.9'2–dc23

  ISBN 978–1–4448–1428–6

Published by
F. A. Thorpe (Publishing)
Anstey, Leicestershire

Set by Words & Graphics Ltd.
Anstey, Leicestershire
Printed and bound in Great Britain by
T. J. International Ltd., Padstow, Cornwall

This book is printed on acid-free paper

Prologue

'My dear Alex, the time has come for you to seek a wife.'

He raised an elegant eyebrow and smiled at Sarah's reflection. 'I do hope you are not . . . applying for the position, Sarah, my love?'

Her generous lips curved and she laughed. 'Good God! You know I cannot bear the country and have no interest whatsoever in children. You may relax, my dear, I have no designs on your inheritance. Nutley left me more money than I can spend in my lifetime.'

She threw back the covers and stepped, unashamed of her voluptuous nakedness, to the floor. 'No, Alex, you spend far too much of your time worrying about your motherless children. So, find yourself a well-bred young woman who prefers the country and adores children and marry her.'

'It's a good suggestion, my darling, but how am I to find such a paragon? I can't imagine any suitable young woman would accept a marriage of convenience with no opportunity to socialise or appear in town during the Season.' Satisfied his neck cloth was arranged as it should be, he reached for his jacket.

'Allow me. This is new, is it not? I think that dark blue a perfect colour for you; it exactly matches your eyes.'

He was tempted to ignore the proffered garment and tumble his delectable companion back between the sheets, but she saw his expression change, dropped his coat into his hand and vanished into her dressing room. She called through the closed door.

'You have an appointment with the Prime Minister and I don't intend to come between you and your duties. Think about what I said, Alex. The Haverstocks' annual house party takes place at the end of the month. I think this an excellent place to start your search.'

'May I call again this week?'

'No, I do not wish to see you until you've found yourself a compliant bride.'

This was the outside of enough. Pushing through the closed door, he strolled into the dressing room where his mistress was luxuriating in a rose-scented bath. 'Do not push me too far, Sarah. I have no intention of being manipulated by you or any other woman.'

'Do not scowl at me, my darling, I did not say you had to be married, merely to have found a girl that will do.'

She was irresistible and she knew it.

'Very well, I shall attend the house party.

But that is as far as I shall go with this nonsensical demand. If there is anyone suitable I shall make them an offer, but if there is not . . . ?'

'I can ask no more of you, my dear. Although I have no fondness for children myself I do not like to think of your three languishing at Blakely Hall with only servants to take care of them.'

Alex knew where this was leading and walked smartly out of the room, closing the door with a decided click. He was not prepared to discuss his lack of parental concern for his children with anyone, and especially not his mistress. When Anna had died giving birth to their fourth child in as many years he had vowed he would never again put a woman in such jeopardy.

His beautiful young wife had been the love of his life. He had left his home, and his three small children, unable to face the future alone. Sarah Nutley's timely intervention had saved his sanity and perhaps his life. She had dragged him from the brink and he was now able to go about in Society, apparently recovered from his grief.

What had not changed was his reluctance to spend time in what had been a place of happiness. He paid duty visits to his offspring, but never remained above one night. His mouth

3

twisted. He blinked back tears. What would Anna think of his lack of concern for her beloved children? His home was an empty shell without her there to share it with him. Snatching up his hat and gloves, he strode from the bedchamber.

Sarah was right to castigate him; Lucy, Elizabeth and Alexander deserved better. He scarcely knew how old they were now. They were paraded in front of him by the nanny and nursemaid and always looked presentable. But were they happy? How could they be, left in the care of servants?

1

'Who is that woman playing with the children, Haverstock?' Lord Alexander Bentley stepped back from the stone balustrade to talk to his host.

'Oh, that one? That is the Lady Eleanor, the younger sister of Edward Thorrington. You know, Edward inherited the title of the Earl of Tendring a few years ago when his father blew out his brains.'

Alex frowned. 'I remember the incident. He had gambled away everything that wasn't entailed, had he not?' He stepped back to stare down at the painfully thin young woman. She was dressed more like a governess than a member of the aristocracy. Her dark hair was scraped back in an ugly arrangement and did nothing to improve her looks.

Sir Reginald Haverstock was hailed by someone inside the billiard room and left Alex alone on the terrace.

Was this the woman he was looking for? He must make further enquiries.

Alex strolled into the billiard room. 'Haverstock, tell me, how many guests are you anticipating?'

His hosts shrugged. 'No idea, Bentley; best ask the wife. But usually we expect to accommodate around forty.'

'Are we to expect a plethora of children?'

'God forbid! No, those four are family. My wife is cousin to Lady Thorrington and we make an exception for her brood.'

★ ★ ★

'Aunt Eleanor, who is that man staring at us? I have not seen him before this,' Ned, her brother's heir, shouted as he caught the ball Jonathan hurled in his direction.

She glanced over her shoulder. A tall, fair, gentleman of aristocratic mien was looking down from the terrace. She straightened from her crouch over the cricket bat. How long had he been there? He must be a recent addition to the gathering as she did not recognise him.

She nodded and the man bowed. Etiquette satisfied, she returned to the lively game she was enjoying with her three nephews and her niece.

'Aunt Eleanor,' Amanda said from behind the stumps, 'that man's coming down. Do you think he wants to join in our game?'

'I doubt it, my dear, but I shall ask him for you. We are desperately in need of another fielder, for the boys are quite worn out fetching back my magnificent hits.'

Her face was glowing and no doubt liberally streaked with dirt, but she did not care. Playing with her charges, away from the stifling atmosphere inside the house, was the only time she was happy. The four children gathered around her. Ned at almost twelve was already old enough to feel himself her protector.

He was the only one she had.

The man approaching was above normal height and not especially broad, but substantial enough not to need extra padding in the shoulders of his jacket. He wore his hair fashionably short and his eyes were an unusual shade of dark blue. He was every inch the aristocrat. What possible reason could there be for him to wish to speak to her?

'I apologize for disturbing your game, Lady Eleanor, but may I be permitted to join you?' He smiled at the children. 'Lord Bentley, at your service, madam.'

Without waiting for a by your leave he removed his jacket, tossing it carelessly to the ground, and then took up a position in the outfield. She had no choice. For some obscure reason, his lordship was now part of the children's game of cricket.

Gathering her wits, she hastily introduced

her niece and nephews. They were in no doubt: his addition to the fielding side was most welcome. Resuming her stance, she braced herself to receive the next ball. She forgot about the unwanted fielder and concentrated on striking the ball cleanly.

'Gracious! Lord Bentley will have to go into the lake to fetch that ball, Aunt Eleanor.'

'Jonathan, you must not let his lordship wade into the water. You run over and fetch it for us.'

'Too late! He's taken his boots off already.'

Ned laughed. 'I doubt he'll find it; you definitely hit a six. I'd better go and assist in the search if we wish to continue the game.'

Eleanor hesitated, not sure if she should join in or remain where she was with Amanda. 'The afternoon is decidedly warm, don't you think? A paddle in the ornamental lake is exactly what we all need to cool us down.

Taking her niece's hand, she ran across the grass to join her nephews who had already removed their stockings and were about to plunge into the shallow water. Lord Bentley had his back to her and was poking about amongst the lilies with the stick he had found on the bank. This was the ideal opportunity for her to remove her own slippers and step into the lake without revealing her bare feet in an unseemly manner.

'Are you coming in as well, Aunt Eleanor?' Ned called out in surprise.

His words caused Lord Bentley to turn sharply and his foot slipped. To her horror, he fell backwards and disappeared under the water. Ned did not hesitate; he jumped in and plunged across to offer his assistance. Peter and Amanda huddled closer to her. She could feel them trembling beside her.

Before she could offer them any reassurance, Lord Bentley emerged wearing a lily pad on his head.

★ ★ ★

Alex felt his feet sliding from under him.

God's teeth!

He was in for a soaking. Fortunately the weather was clement and the water warm. He pushed himself upright but found his passage obstructed by the plants which grew in profusion in the water. Grabbing the stems of the offending lilies, he wrenched them from the bottom of the lake and stood up, knowing his appearance dressed in greenery would cause much hilarity.

Why were they not laughing? The oldest boy was at his side, his face pinched with fear.

'My lord, it wasn't Aunt Eleanor's fault; it was mine.'

'It was nobody's fault; it was an accident. Here, help me remove these plants from my head. I must look like King Canute dressed as I am.' He laughed heartily and deliberately tripped the boy up, making him as wet as he was.

He glanced for a second time at the tableau on the bank and was relieved that his antics had removed the look of terror from their faces. 'Come on in, we haven't found that wretched ball yet, and I refuse to leave this place until we have it.'

'Go along, children, join Lord Bentley. I shall remain here and watch you play.'

Immediately Alex was surrounded by gambolling children and the search for the missing cricket ball was soon abandoned in splashing and jumping. He wished the pale girl on the bank felt able to join in, but she was constantly glancing over her shoulder as if expecting to be reprimanded for allowing the children to get wet.

He reached down and scooped up the child. 'Well, my little mermaid, I think you must return to your aunt. Come along, boys, I shall replace the ball myself. We will resume our game of cricket tomorrow.'

'This has been capital fun, sir. Normally we

should not have been allowed to . . . ' Ned's voice trailed away but his meaning was clear.

'There will be no repercussions, young man, on any of you. I shall speak to your father and explain the circumstances.'

The look of relief on the boy's face told him everything.

'My lord, I must thank you for playing with the children. I can't remember when they last had such fun. If you would speak to my brother, I should be most grateful. I do not wish the children to be blamed in any way for ruining their clothes.'

'I have not met Lord Thorrington. Has Lady Thorrington accompanied her husband here?'

'Yes, sir, but she and Lady Haverstock, have gone into the village this afternoon.'

'In which case I suggest we return to our chambers and change.' He surveyed the dripping group in front of him, and his heart lurched. Did his own children ever get the opportunity to play cricket or lark about in *his* ornamental lake? Time he took matters in hand. Four long years had passed since Anna died. She would be disappointed in him for ignoring the little ones she had adored.

Lady Eleanor curtsied. The little girl copied her and the three boys bowed. 'Thank you, Lord Bentley, for making the children's afternoon so wonderful. I shall look forward to meeting you here tomorrow to resume our game of cricket.'

With the children close beside her, almost as if they were protecting her from harm, she hurried off to the house. He picked up his boots and stockings and walked across the grass to collect his jacket. When he turned to follow them, they had already vanished.

Deliberately, he chose to re-enter the abbey via the billiard room as Thorrington had been expected there. There was something worrying about the behaviour of the children and their aunt and he intended to make it his business to find out what it was.

Alex's appearance at the billiard room window was greeted by exclamations of horror and amusement. A man he did not recognize viewed him with disfavour. Could this be Thorrington?

'I beg your pardon, gentlemen, but I had a mishap in the lake and four delightful children rushed to my rescue.' He bowed feeling slightly ridiculous as the water pooled about his bare feet. 'I believe they might be your offspring, sir. Are you Thorrington by any chance?'

'I am. And you are?'

'Bentley, at your service. Lady Eleanor was most upset that the children got wet, but I

12

assured her the soaking was in a good cause.'

The earl did not return his smile. 'I do not approve of children putting themselves forward in this way. I shall have words with my sister on the matter.'

'I hope you will not, Thorrington. As I have just told you, if fault there was, then I shall claim it.'

The other man did not reply, but nodded and resumed his game. Alex felt a surge of anger. There was nothing more he could do now, but as soon as he was changed he would take the man to one side and make his point as forcibly as necessary. Neither the children nor their aunt would be admonished for what took place this afternoon or there would be repercussions of a different sort, and directed entirely at Thorrington.

★ ★ ★

'Hurry up! We shall take the back stairs; we are less likely to be observed if we do.'

Eleanor thanked God her sister-in-law was absent for the afternoon. With luck this escapade would go unremarked. She shivered at the thought of what might happen if Jane reported the matter to her brother.

The nursery had been given over to the exclusive use of the Thorrington children and

13

herself. The Haverstock offspring were grown and no longer had need of it. The two nursery maids greeted their appearance with dismay.

'Look at the state of you! You'll catch your death of cold if we don't get you out of your wet garments.'

'Thank you, Betty. The children were assisting Lord Bentley in his search for the cricket ball which unfortunately ended up in the lake.' Eleanor decided it would be wise to mention his name straight away to make the episode seem more acceptable.

'We can manage ourselves, Betty. I shall help Peter with his buttons,' Jonathan said.

'Thank you, sir, that's most kind of you. Mary and I shall take care of Lady Amanda.'

'Excellent; then I can change my gown whilst you do so. I think it best if we remain upstairs for the remainder of the day. Shall we play hide and go seek in the attics once we are clean and dry again?'

Her suggestion was greeted by a chorus of delight. Even five-year-old Amanda enjoyed this game, as long as she was allowed to hide and seek with Eleanor. Betty handed the little girl over to her junior.

'I shall launder the clothes myself, Lady Eleanor. I promise you word of this will not leave the nursery.'

'Lord Bentley has said he will speak to my

brother so I am hopeful there will be no unpleasant repercussions. I shall keep the children out of sight until tomorrow. If anyone saw us by the lake, hopefully, by then, they will have forgotten about it.'

The maid smiled sympathetically. 'Leave your gown out and I will have it clean and ready to wear by tomorrow, my lady.'

Eleanor was fortunate to have the support of Betty and Mary. Without them her life would be intolerable.

2

The afternoon passed pleasantly enough but Eleanor jumped every time a door opened or she heard footsteps in the passage. The children were washing their hands, ready for nursery tea, when the footmen arrived with a message demanding that she go downstairs immediately to her sister-in-law's apartment. She prayed Jane was the one who wished to speak to her, not her brother.

'I hope I shall not be long. Betty, give the children their meal immediately it arrives. Don't let it go cold on my account.'

'What shall I tell them if they ask where you are?'

'Just say that I have come down to the library to find a fresh book to read to them before they go to bed.'

She was familiar with the house, having stayed there several times before. This was the third time she'd been summoned to the first floor since arriving three days ago. Hopefully Jane wished to speak to her on some other matter and not about the interlude at the lake.

She paused outside the door to check that

her hair was pulled back correctly and her dress was free of cobwebs from her scrambling around the attics. She knocked firmly on the sitting-room door.

Her heart sank. Her brother bid her come in.

'You took your time. Fifteen minutes have passed since I sent for you.'

Eleanor did not apologize for it made little difference to his treatment of her. If he was in a mind to be brutal, nothing she or Jane could say would deflect him. At least he had not managed to break her spirit or cause her to lose her self-respect. She shuddered to think what might happen to her if she ever removed her dowry from his keeping. The interest was all he had to live on much of the time.

'Well, I am here now. I am about to serve the children's meal. You would not wish them to eat cold food, I am sure.'

'I don't give a damn about their food.' He strode across the room and she braced herself for a blow, but he stopped and grabbed her wrist instead, twisting it cruelly.

'What is this I hear about cavorting in the lake?'

She stared back at him, determined not to flinch. 'Lord Bentley fell in and the children went to assist him. *He* was no way discommoded by the experience. In fact, he positively enjoyed being wet.'

He dropped her arm and stepped away. 'If I have any reports of misbehaviour from any of my children you know what to expect. Either you shall be the whipping boy or I shall thrash each of them in turn.'

'Will that be all?'

He didn't answer but gestured towards the door. She turned and made a dignified exit, relieved she had escaped with nothing worse than a bruised wrist. His threat was not an idle one; she had received two beatings in the last six months in order to protect the children.

She stumbled to the window seat at the far end of the corridor.

How much longer could she endure this punishment? Why didn't Jane protest?

Hating a member of her family was wrong, but her brother was an evil man, a gambler and drinker like their father had been before him. He was deeply in debt again. The only time he came home was when he was insolvent. The longer he stayed, the worse his treatment of his family became.

Her face was wet and her nose running; she could not return to the nursery until she was more composed.

'Here, Lady Eleanor, take this.'

To her astonishment, Lord Bentley pushed a soft white handkerchief into her hand and then joined her on the seat whilst she mopped her face.

'I did not hear you approaching, my lord. I'm sorry that you should see me like this. I thank you for the handkerchief.' She blew her nose and pushed the soiled item to her pocket, knowing better than to offer to return it.

'Your wrist was not bruised like that earlier in the day. Who did that to you?'

Her eyes flew up in horror. He must not intervene on her behalf, it would make matters so much worse. 'This is nothing, sir, a rough game with the children and I came off the loser. I bruise more easily than most.'

His eyes were sympathetic, and he did not press the point. 'I look forward to seeing you at dinner, Lady Eleanor.'

'Oh no! I do not dine downstairs. I eat with the children in the nursery. If you will excuse me, my lord, I must be getting back or my meal will be cold.'

★   ★   ★

Alex watched the young woman vanish through the servants' door. His fists clenched. No child's fingers had caused those marks.

Thorrington had done it, he was sure.

God's teeth! Eleanor was the daughter of an earl, not a poor relation or a serving wench. She should be dining downstairs with the other guests.

He would speak to Haverstock and enquire politely why she did not join them. Thorrington might take precedence in the matter of titles, but the Bentley fortune was such that when it came to influence what Alex wanted would be arranged. Having friends in Government was useful in a situation like this.

As he was changing, his mind drifted back to Sarah. He wished she could accompany him to these parties, but Society frowned on women who chose to go their own way.

Was Eleanor the kind of person his mistress had in mind when she had sent him on this quest for a wife? What were the requirements? Impeccable breeding, submissive, and a love of children — good grief! He had found someone that fitted this description exactly. He would prefer someone a little more prepossessing, but as he had no intention of sharing his bed with her, her lack of countenance was no handicap.

She appeared to have a lively wit; however little time he intended to spend with his wife, he could not marry a simpleton. Tomorrow he would spend the afternoon with her and the children playing cricket and get to know her better.

Alex strolled into the drawing-room to find it all but empty of guests. The glass doors at the far end of the room had been thrown open and everyone was outside enjoying the early evening sunshine. No, not quite everyone, a small nervous woman was hiding in the depths of an armchair.

'Excuse me, madam, but are you unwell? Can I send for your abigail to assist you?'

The woman shook her head. 'No, thank you, Lord Bentley. I am perfectly content to remain here where I shall not be disturbed.'

He bowed. 'You have the advantage of me, madam. I do not believe we have been introduced.'

'I am Lady Thorrington. I believe you have already met my sister-in-law, Lady Eleanor.'

'May I join you? I have no wish to socialise either.'

She nodded, glancing at the door before answering. 'Please do, my lord. But you will find me poor company; you would be much better entertained outside.'

Flicking aside his tails, he folded himself into a chair opposite. 'I met your children as well as your sister-in-law today. They are delightful bunch of youngsters. You must be

21

very proud of them.'

Her face lit up. 'Oh, I cannot tell you how much I love them. Thorrington prefers that Eleanor take care of them so they do not have a governess. I believe she is responsible for them being so charming and well-behaved.'

'I am surprised Lady Eleanor is not to join us tonight. This is a most unusual circumstance; surely a member of the aristocracy shouldn't be kept apart from society in this way? I should like to further my acquaintance with her. I rarely meet young ladies of intelligence.'

She gasped and her fingers tore at her reticule. 'Oh, Lord Bentley, you must not mention it. My husband would not be pleased if you showed an interest in her. She is indispensable to the family and has no wish to leave us.' Lady Thorrington pushed herself upright. 'Pray, excuse me, sir. I must join my husband outside.'

He watched her go; his brow creased. There was more to this business than he had at first surmised. He had no wish to make Lady Eleanor's life more difficult, but was curious as to why this plain young woman allowed herself to be mistreated. She must have had at least one Season. She was not an antidote exactly, so why had she not been taken?

As Lady Thorrington had been so insistent he did not enquire after her sister-in-law he decided not to speak to Haverstock. Tomorrow he would seek out Lady Eleanor and discover what kept her tied to her brother's household. Did she have no dowry? Perhaps that was the problem. However well-bred, a plain woman without money would not be sought after as a bride.

★ ★ ★

'I think that is enough for this morning, children. You have worked hard. You may put your books away.'

'Are we to play cricket again, Aunt Eleanor?'

'No, my love, I thought we could take a picnic to the woods. We are becoming uncomfortably hot up here and I am sure that the lawns will be unpleasant too.'

She decided to take Mary with her, that way she was less likely to be accosted by anyone. It would be an unmitigated disaster if Bentley decided to take an interest in her welfare. His interference would push her brother into further unpleasantness. At least if Edward was bullying *her*, he was leaving his children unmolested. Poor Jane was another matter.

She had no intention of committing the folly of marrying; not that any man would offer for her now. She was approaching five and twenty, and had lost what looks she had been blessed with. If there was any way to remove herself from her brother's control she would take it, but without her inheritance, she was as dependent on him as his wife and children.

'We shall take the back stairs as usual, children. Try not to clatter with your boots on the boards; we do not wish to disturb anyone.' They all knew she meant not alert their father.

Outside there was not a cloud in the sky. Hopefully it would be cooler in the woods. Male voices were approaching from the stables.

'Quickly, let us race to the path that leads into the wood. Amanda and I shall go first, then Peter, then Jonathan, and last Ned. Remember, you must count to twenty after each person departs before the next one can leave.' She smiled at Mary. 'I do not expect you to run but follow on at your own pace.'

Taking the little girl's hand, she gathered her skirts and set off, shortening her strides to accommodate the child beside her. The laughs and shouts of the boys as they ran behind lifted her spirits and, as always, they arrived at roughly the same time.

'That was capital, Aunt Eleanor. I'm quite puffed out. I need to sit down in the shade for a bit.'

'If you recall, Ned, there's a stream not far ahead; if we walk there we can dip our toes in the water to cool down.'

'I'm thirsty. Can we drink the water?' Amanda asked.

'As long as we drink before we paddle, I'm sure it will be perfectly safe. The stream crosses the paddocks after it leaves the woods.'

Mary arrived, red-faced and out of breath. 'Well, I never! I've been eating too many puddings. I don't run as fast as I used to.'

'Never mind, Mary. You had to carry the picnic so it wasn't a fair race. We are going to the stream for a drink and you can have a paddle with us.' Ned grinned and held out his hand to take the basket but Mary shook her head.

'Why, thank you, Lord Edward, I might just do that.'

Eleanor settled her charges along the edge of the bank and demonstrated how they could scoop water up in their cupped hands. This enterprise was fraught with difficulty and by the time they had quenched their thirst they were weak with laughter and considerably damper than when they had begun.

'There, that was fun, wasn't it, children? Shall we sit in the sun until our clothes are dry?'

'I want to paddle, Aunt Eleanor. So what's the use of getting dry as we are all going to get wet again?'

'Excellent point, Jonathan. But please, all of you, don't fall in. Your father was not impressed by our activities yesterday.'

She hated to dampen their enthusiasm but soon her brother would not be satisfied with chastising her. He would begin disciplining his children as well. Her pleasure in the excursion was gone. She smiled as though she was enjoying herself and stood, watching them paddle.

'I shall go in with them, Lady Eleanor, you sit under the trees and rest a while.'

'Thank you, Mary, I didn't sleep well last night and shall certainly enjoy a quiet sit down after all that exertion.'

Eleanor took the picnic with her into the shade. Everyone was dressed in their oldest garments so there was no harm in sitting on the grass. She settled comfortably, her back against a tree trunk, and closed her eyes, letting the peace of the woodland restore her jangled nerves.

★ ★ ★

Alex was returning from the stables with his host and two other gentlemen when he saw Eleanor and the children running across the grass to the woods. A plump nursemaid trundled along behind, clutching a picnic basket. The shouts and calls from the boys made him smile. The adults in that household were either subdued or bad-tempered, but the children were obviously unaffected, their high spirits plain to see.

'Forgive me, Haverstock, I have left my crop behind. I shall, no doubt, catch up with you in the billiard room later this afternoon.'

He let the others continue without him and headed for the woods. Lady Eleanor was chaperoned so it would be perfectly accept-able for him to join her and children for a while even in the privacy of the trees.

The sound of splashing echoed down the path. What was it about this family and water? Smiling, he headed towards the noise. However, something made him pause, to dawdle, giving him time to consider the real reason he was seeking out her company.

He needed a mother for his children, not a wife. Sarah gave him everything that a wife could, and made no demands either financial or emotional. The arrangement suited him

27

perfectly. He had known when he met Anna that he would never love another. Eleanor would be an ideal choice for what he required. Surely she would leap at the chance to escape from her brother's cruel domination? All he had to do was spend the day with her and he would know for certain if she was a suitable candidate.

The shouting and laughter drew him forward but the voice talking to the children was that of the nursemaid, not Eleanor. Soft footed, he approached the sunlit clearing just ahead, wanting to see before being seen.

The children were paddling in the stream, lifting stones and exclaiming over what they discovered hiding there. Where was their aunt? A slight movement at the far side of the dell caught his eye and he moved forward. His quarry was resting peacefully against a tree trunk, her skirt smoothed out carefully over her legs and not even an inch of ankle visible. He remained where he was for a moment staring at her. She looked almost pretty with the harsh lines of worry smoothed from her face.

He must not lurk in this way. He cleared his throat loudly. 'Lady Eleanor, is there sufficient in your hamper to feed an extra mouth?'

Her eyes flew open and there was dismay,

not pleasure, written on her face. He was not wanted here; he had made a grave error of judgement. He bowed. 'I beg your pardon, madam. I am obviously *de trop*. I shall — '

Although he had spoken quietly his words had carried and the smallest boy heard him. 'Lord Bentley, what fun! Are you going to fall in the stream for us today?'

He shrugged an apology and turned to greet the child. 'Absolutely not! However, I shall be delighted to paddle with you all. Do you know how to catch a stickleback with your hands?'

'I am sorry if I seemed ungracious, sir, you startled me. You are, of course, most welcome to stay and enjoy a picnic with us.'

He glanced down, Eleanor was smiling, but it didn't reach her eyes. His first impression had been correct; she did not want him here. She was prepared to suffer his presence because the children wished it. For some reason her disdain annoyed him. He did not enjoy being rebuffed in this way.

3

When Eleanor opened her eyes and saw Bentley standing there, her stomach flipped. Why was this man pursuing her? She had no wish to encourage him; the last time a gentleman had shown a serious interest in her he had vanished without a trace. It might have been a coincidence, but she feared her brother had been involved with his disappearance. She had no wish to be responsible for any harm coming to this man just because he felt sorry for her and enjoyed the company of the children.

She had not intended to reveal her feelings, but his smile faded. Hastily scrambling to her feet, she went to his side to tender her apologies. Now that Peter had seen him, she had no choice but to invite him to stay. Should she warn him of her fears or would he think her ready for Bedlam?

Of course she couldn't speak. Not only would he consider her deranged, but would think her decidedly forward. She was at her last prayers — of what possible interest could she be to this handsome aristocrat? From the cut of his clothes, one could see he spared no expense. Haverstock only invited the cream of Society to his house parties.

At his mention of catching sticklebacks her interest was piqued. 'That is impossible, sir. They are the smallest and most slippery of creatures. I defy anyone to catch one in his hands.'

He grinned. 'Is that a challenge? I accept. But I shall demand a reward if I am successful.'

'Nonsense! You shall have my resounding applause and that will have to suffice.'

'Very well, Lady Eleanor. However, you must promise to answer me three questions honestly if I succeed, and I shall do the same for you if I fail. Is that acceptable?'

There seemed no harm in this request so she nodded. 'I agree. Now, children, we must set some rules for this challenge. How many attempts is Lord Bentley to be allowed before we declare him the loser?'

'Three, no more, but you may take as long as you like for each one, my lord.' Ned, as always, acted as spokesperson for his siblings. The boys clapped and Amanda squealed.

'Hush, children, your noise is scaring away the fish. We do not wish to be unfair to Lord Bentley, now do we?'

'I don't believe fish have ears, Lady Eleanor. As long as no one splashes about in

31

the water whilst I make my attempts you may make as much noise as you wish.'

Eleanor turned to Mary, who was standing to one side and most interested in what was taking place. 'Would you lay out the picnic under the tree, please, Mary? We shall all be hungry and thirsty by the time this fish catching experiment is over.'

Lord Bentley lay face down on the bank and peered into the shallow water where the reeds and stones were plentiful. She watched with amazement as one by one the children lay down on either side of him, mesmerized by his strange behaviour. Intrigued in spite of her reservations, she stood behind him, watching what he did.

He pushed himself onto his knees with a satisfied smile. 'This is an ideal spot. I must remove my jacket and roll up my shirtsleeves before I attempt this amazing feat. Young man, do you have a receptacle in which I can put my trophy?'

Peter scrambled to his feet and delved into his pockets. 'I have my handkerchief. Will that do?'

Ned laughed derisively. 'A handkerchief, Peter? Lord Bentley means a jar of some sort, do you not, sir?'

'Your handkerchief will do perfectly. If you soak it first, the fish will come to no harm the short time it will be out of the water.'

Eleanor followed Bentley as he walked away from the edge of the stream to remove his jacket. 'Thank you. I'm afraid that sometimes Ned can be a little harsh in his dealings with his younger brothers. He does not suffer fools gladly.' She could have added he had more reason to be aggressive than the other three, but refrained. How the children behaved was none of this man's business. What went on in her family was a private matter.

Mary hurried across to take his jacket, carefully draping it over a convenient branch. When Eleanor turned he was beside the water, his shirt sleeves rolled up. She flushed. Surely a man should not be displaying his forearms? Should she not go and join him at the bank? Ignoring the possible breach of etiquette she hurried over to stand as before, just behind him. The children resumed their places, prone on the grassy edge.

The only sounds in the dell were the gurgle of the water and the songs of the birds in the trees that surrounded them. The children had never been so quiet or remained so still. She peered over his shoulder as his strong brown arm slipped into the water. He held it stationary for a few moments. Then with a flick of his wrist, a small scrap of wriggling silver flew into the air to land at her feet. Immediately Peter was beside it and rolled it tenderly into his wet handkerchief.

'Good gracious! That was amazing! Look children, before we put it back. Isn't it a beautiful fish?' She had no need to urge them for they were already exclaiming in admiration. Peter, who had taken charge of the stickleback, decided it had been out of its element long enough and tipped it back. The fish swam away unharmed.

'I believe I have just won the challenge, Lady Eleanor. Shall we stroll around the wood whilst the children attempt to emulate my amazing skill?'

The last thing she wanted was to be private with him. If Jane or Edward learnt of this there would be horrible repercussions not only for herself but also for Lord Bentley. 'I cannot leave the children alone at the water's edge, my lord. We shall have to postpone questioning until another time.'

He was not so easily dissuaded. 'Mary, come and watch the children. Lady Eleanor and I wish to sit under the tree and converse.'

The maid curtsied and rushed to obey his command. How dare he issue orders to her servants? 'I am sorry, Lord Bentley, but I'm no longer amused by this silly charade. I think it would be better if you return to the abbey.' She nodded her dismissal and his jaw hardened. 'I am sure you would not wish to be the subject of idle gossip any more than I would.'

He snatched up his jacket and attempted to ram his arms in without bothering to roll down his shirt sleeves. The top coat was close-fitting. This was an impossible task.

He had his back to her. Should she offer to help before he lost his temper and blamed her, or one of the children, for his plight?

She shrank back against the tree. He spun around and she flinched.

⋆ ⋆ ⋆

God's teeth!

Alex was firmly jammed, both arms half in his jacket and unable to extricate himself. His lips twitched. This ridiculous situation had put paid to his storming off in high dudgeon. He would have to ask for her assistance or he would be stuck there like a clodpole when the children came for their lunch. No doubt she would be laughing already at his predicament.

He turned and his amusement faded.

What had happened to turn a confident young woman into a shivering heap? 'What is it? What has frightened you?'

There must be something in the trees. He could not protect her, restricted as he was. He would be free regardless of the ruination of his new jacket. He punched his arms out and heard a shocking rip as the sleeves tore from the shoulder seams, leaving him unfettered.

He froze. He could hear his breathing in the silence. The children had stopped playing, Lady Eleanor was clutching the trunk of the tree for support. Angrily he ripped the sleeves from his arms and tossed them down. He must reassure her, tell her he would not let anything harm her. He took one step forwards and then a small body launched itself onto his back knocking him to his knees.

'You shall not harm her. You're a bad man. I hate you. I hate you.' Each statement was accompanied by punches and kicks. Fortunately the youngster was still barefoot. Alex reached round and gripped Ned's arms, swinging him around to face him.

'Enough. Enough, young man.' He shook the boy to emphasize his command. From nowhere Eleanor appeared, a length of stick in her hand. There was a searing pain in his head and his world went black.

*   *   *

Eleanor dropped the piece of wood she had used to strike Lord Bentley. She was frozen to the spot. Her limbs were leaden. She felt as if she was viewing the unconscious man through the wrong end of a spyglass. Amanda whimpered and her brain refocused.

'I have not killed him, darling, he shall be perfectly fine in a little while.' She had no idea if this was in fact the case. He had fallen as if pole-axed. Unless she turned him over to view the injury she would have no idea if the damage was as serious as it appeared. Ned was not so squeamish.

'He is still breathing, Aunt Eleanor, but there is a prodigious amount of blood. What are we going to do?'

The children must go back to the house. They could not be involved in this disaster. 'Mary, quickly, take the children away. If you follow this path it will lead you to the maze. Take them in there and don't return to the abbey for an hour at least. Pretend you have been there all morning. I shall deal with this matter.'

She guided the children back to the stream and helped Mary refasten their boots. Gathering them within the circle of arms she kissed each in turn. 'My dears, you must not speak of this to anyone — ever. Do you understand? Whatever happens to me, this has nothing to do with any of you. I can only bear the consequences of my actions if I know that you are all safe.'

Amanda dried her eyes on her sleeve and Peter sniffed loudly. The two older boys exchanged worried glances, but nodded their agreement. Ned said what they were all thinking. 'I didn't think there could be another gentleman with the same temper as our father. Whatever anyone says, he deserved it.'

Eleanor squeezed Ned's shoulder. 'You're brave, young man. I am proud of you. You must now take care of your siblings. I love you, all of you. God bless you.'

She remained on her knees until they were out of sight. Would this be the last time she ever saw them? She had not known herself to be a violent woman. Her repressed rage had surfaced in a moment of madness when she had seen Bentley about to hurt her nephew.

Bandages were needed and a clean wet cloth to clean the wound. When she had tended to the injured man she would run to the house and fetch help. To leave him to die was unthinkable even if his recovery would mean her possible arrest and certain incarceration.

Would it be better to claim insanity and be confined to an institution or tell the truth and pray that the magistrate would believe her? She shuddered. Would her title protect her from the hangman's noose if poor Lord Bentley died?

After tearing several strips from her petticoat she dipped one into the stream to clean the wound. She must not procrastinate further. This man had not deserved to be struck down. Her eyes brimmed. He had children of his own. What would the poor things do if they were left orphaned by her dreadful actions?

He was so still; he had not moved nor made a sound since she had hit him on the forehead. Dropping to her knees beside him, she placed her fingers at the juncture of his jawbone and his neck. To her astonishment, and relief, she felt a regular pulse. Lord Bentley was alive, and perhaps not as badly injured as she had feared.

With some difficulty she rolled him over. The gash running across the right-hand side of his head made her stomach lurch. He must have lost half a pint of blood already and if she did nothing to stem the flow he would die. Folding the wet material, she cleaned away the traces of bark and dirt from the wound then quickly pressed a second pad across the gash.

Holding this in place, she deftly tied several

strips of petticoat around his head and didn't release the pressure until she was certain the bandages were doing the job for her. Throughout this procedure he had been comatose, his breathing regular, but he showed no sign of waking. Satisfied she had done all she could, she ran across to fetch the picnic rug and placed it over him. Retrieving the sleeves from his coat she folded them up and put them carefully under his head.

There was nothing more she could do.

Her gown was blood-spattered, no doubt her face and hands also. Would it help to clean herself and appear at the abbey calm and dispassionate? Or would running pellmell to report her crime in her dishevelled state give weight to her plea of insanity? The blood-stained cloths she had used were scattered on the grass. She could not bear to look at them. When they were safely buried she was ready to return and report what had happened.

The strain of the past thirty minutes caught up with her and her knees folded. She collapsed under the tree, unable to stop the violent trembling. She drew her knees into her chest and wrapped her arms around them as if by holding on tight she could prevent this catastrophe from overwhelming her. Why had she not reserved this rage for her brother?

If Ned had not attacked Bentley, she was sure he would have done no more than shout at her.

Perhaps it would not hurt if she remained where she was a moment longer. This was her last opportunity to breathe in the sweet scents of the countryside before she was taken away by the constables. When her head stopped spinning and her limbs remained still she would check once more on the patient and then fetch assistance.

Slowly her wits returned and she inched her way up the tree trunk until straight. She stumbled across to the man she had so grievously injured and stooped to check his pulse. Relieved to find his skin was warmer and his heart beating firmly, she straightened.

With one final glance around the clearing, she turned and hurried back along the path. She rehearsed several versions of the event but could think of none that would serve. Unless she involved the children or suggested that Lord Bentley had made an unprovoked attack on her chastity, there was no explanation that made sense.

When she arrived at the rear of the house she came face-to-face with her host. Haverstock's shocked expression reminded her she had neglected to remove the blood from her person.

'My dear child, what has happened? Has there been an accident?'

She found she couldn't speak. The enormity of what she'd done completely overwhelmed her.

'Lord Bentley — in the woods.'

She managed no more before collapsing into welcoming blackness.

4

Alex opened his eyes to find himself alone in the woods. What the hell had happened? His memory was fuzzy and his head hurt like the very devil. He could remember nothing after deciding to follow Lady Eleanor and the children. He had obviously been injured and someone had tended to his wound.

Gingerly he touched his forehead. His fingers encountered a neatly wrapped bandage. How extraordinary! What had happened to the sleeves of his jacket? Who had covered him up with a picnic blanket? He wished he could recall how he had come to be injured. He must assume that Lady Eleanor had been the one to look after him, but why had she left him alone?

He should get up, not lie on the ground waiting for someone to assist him. He pushed himself up to his elbows and a wave of nausea accompanied by a blinding pain across his eyes sent him plunging back into oblivion.

★   ★   ★

The next time he regained consciousness, he was in bed and a doctor stood beside him.

'Lord Bentley, I am Dr Smith. I am going to remove your bandages and suture your wound.'

'Is it that bad? I can remember nothing. I have no idea how I received the injury.'

'Judging by the quantities of blood upon your person I imagine you have a serious gash. If you are ready, I shall begin my treatment.'

The doctor did not speak to him again. In fact, his whole manner was brusque to the point of rudeness. As Alex drifted in and out of consciousness, he tried to force his wandering mind back to the events that had caused the damage to his head. The whole procedure left him faint. He was glad to see the physician depart and be replaced by his valet, Foster.

'Foster, tell me, how did I come by this injury?'

His man looked grave and shook his head. 'Lady Eleanor struck you with a piece of wood. She is too distraught to explain her reasons.'

Lady Eleanor? God's teeth!

He was more confused than ever. Why on earth should this young woman make an unprovoked attack on him? 'I can remember nothing. I followed Lady Eleanor and the children into the wood, but my mind is blank from that point onward.'

'The children spent the morning in the maze with their nursemaid. Lady Eleanor took a picnic hamper into the wood to spend time alone enjoying the countryside.'

Alex closed his eyes. Why was his valet too being so stiff? Like Smith, Foster was showing no sympathy for his master. Apparently, everyone considered the attack to be his fault. A most terrible explanation occurred to him.

There could only be one possible reason why a quiet, nervous young woman should be so desperate as to knock him out.

He had to face it. Was it possible he had tried to force his attentions on Lady Eleanor and she had protected herself in the only way available? He had never raised a hand to a woman or child. He would never hurt someone weaker than himself. So why had she done it? He must have . . . he couldn't complete the thought.

Such an act would explain the way he was being treated, as though he was a social pariah not a well-respected peer of the realm. 'Foster, did I attempt to . . . did I force my attentions on Lady Eleanor?'

'There is no other explanation, Lord

Bentley. If you require anything, sir, I shall be sitting close by.'

Despair overwhelmed him. That poor woman, had she not enough to endure from the bastard Thorrington without him adding to her problems? He was certain he had intended her no harm; she must have misinterpreted his overtures. Somehow he must get on to his feet and put things right. He had almost decided to make her an offer before his appalling behaviour. Now he had no choice.

'Foster, I need to get up. I must see Lady Eleanor.' He tried but got no further than his elbows before a wave of pain and sickness overwhelmed him. When he had recovered sufficiently to think clearly he knew he must write to her, he was in no state to approach her in person.

'Fetch writing materials. If you hold my hand steady I think I can manage to pen a note.'

'Would it not be easier, my lord, for you to dictate and me to act as scribe?'

What the hell! His man knew more about him than any living soul. He would trust him with his life, why not let him do this?

'Very well, get yourself organized whilst I marshal my thoughts.'

The chamber was dark, and for a moment Eleanor was disoriented. Then she remembered everything and her throat tightened as tears spilt down her cheeks.

'My dear Eleanor, do not cry. That monster did not harm you. Thank God you were able to protect yourself from his outrageous attack.'

'Jane? Why are you here? I don't understand, who attacked me?'

Her sister-in-law patted her hand and stepped away to talk quietly to someone Eleanor could not see. 'Kitty, this is far worse than we feared. Poor Eleanor does not even remember what took place. The event was so upsetting she has blanked it out. I am so relieved that Thorrington has gone to Town this morning; he would have been most displeased.'

Edward was away; that was indeed the only good thing about this morning's activities. The ladies obviously thought that an unknown assailant had attacked both her and Lord Bentley, so she would do nothing to disabuse them.

'Jane, how is Lord Bentley?'

'He will recover, but you must not consider him. Dr Smith says you have had a great shock and must rest quietly for the remainder of the day. Is there anything that you need?'

'No, thank you. I should like to sleep, I'm sure I shall feel more the thing when I wake up again.'

'Here, my dear, I shall place this little brass bell on your bedside table. You can ring it if you need assistance of any sort. Lady Haverstock has supplied you with a girl; she is in the dressing room and will hear you easily.'

Eleanor realized she was no longer in the little attic room she always used on their visits. For some reason she was now in a guest chamber, not as grand as some, but twice the size of her usual abode. As soon as she was certain she was alone, she pushed the covers back and climbed out of bed.

A pretty wrapper was draped across the end of the bed. She recognized it as one of Jane's. Things were becoming more strange by the minute. Her sister was not in the habit of lending out her garments in this way. Why was she being treated so royally? Was this like a condemned man's last supper?

Even with the shutters closed she could see how well appointed the chamber was. She was not accustomed to such luxury and having it thrust upon her now made her feel even worse. She did not deserve to be treated well; she was little better than a murderer.

A tap on the door, too soft to be heard by the girl in the dressing room, stopped her maudlin thoughts. Without thinking she walked across to open it. She did not know who was more startled — the smart grey-haired gentleman or herself. He recovered first.

'Lady Eleanor, I have a note for you from Lord Bentley. Would you be so gracious as to read it? I shall remain outside for your response.'

The letter was thrust into her hand, the man bowed, stepped smartly back and closed the door. Her hands were shaking. Why should Bentley wish to write to her? Taking the missive over to the window she pulled open the shutter a little to allow in some sunlight. She unfolded the paper and stared at the contents incredulously.

Lady Eleanor,

I do most heartily beg your forgiveness for my atrocious behaviour. I have no excuses and no explanations. I wish to make amends in the only way open to me. Would you do me the honour of becoming my wife? I knew as soon as I saw you that you were the lady I was seeking.

If you agree, I shall send to London for a

special licence and we can be married tomorrow.

I shall make no demands on you. I wish ours to be a marriage of convenience. I can offer you a comfortable home, a life free from stress and fear and the freedom to live in the countryside.

All I require in return is that you love my children and be a mother to them.

Yours in sincerity,
Alexander Bentley

She read it a second time and the note still said the same thing.

He was apologising to *her*?

Good grief!

All he had done was *threaten* her with violence. *She* should be on her knees begging *his* forgiveness.

Marriage? This was something she had vowed she would never contemplate, but his offer was quite specific. She would be a wife in name only, a mother to his children, and was to remain in the country to live as she pleased.

This proposal beggared belief. She had struck him down and he wished to marry her to make amends? His offer made no sense at all, but he was giving her a lifeline, a means of escaping from her degradation. She must accept; she might never have another chance.

Running to the door, she flung it open to find the messenger pacing up and down as if expecting a curt rejection. 'Do you know the contents of this letter?'

The man nodded.

'In which case you may tell Lord Bentley that I am stunned by his offer, but agree. If he is to obtain a special licence, he will need my details. I do not wish you to apply to Lady Thorrington. I wish no one to know of this arrangement until the marriage has taken place.'

'Thank you, Lady Eleanor. If you could be so kind as to write your details on the back of the letter I shall give the information to Lord Bentley straight away. I shall be travelling to London to obtain the licence. Would you prefer if I brought a curate with me to perform the ceremony?'

'Yes, indeed. It would not do to alert the local vicar of our plans.'

After Bentley's manservant had departed with the necessary dates and facts Eleanor curled up on the bed trying to make sense of what was nonsensical. Another thing that had struck her as odd was the fact that Foster had not quibbled about her desire to keep the matter secret. Did Bentley know that her brother would do everything he could to prevent the union?

The sound of the dressing room door opening woke her from a fitful doze. She sat up to see a smiling maid approaching with a tray. Her stomach gurgled. She had not realized she was so hungry. The hands on the mantel clock were indistinct, but she was fairly sure it must be dinner time.

'I am delighted to see you, I have no idea of the time, but my digestion is telling me many hours have passed since I broke my fast.'

'Shall I put the tray on the table by the window, my lady? If I draw back just one of the shutters you shall have sufficient light to eat your meal.'

'Let me do that, I'm not an invalid. I feel perfectly well, but I do not wish to go downstairs tonight.'

With the shutters pulled back the girl had no difficulty putting down her burden. When she'd done so, she curtsied. 'Cook says if there's nothing here that you fancy, I'm to go down and tell her and she will prepare it for you.'

'Whatever you have fetched will be more than adequate. What is your name? If you are to take care of me I would like to address you personally.'

The girl dipped a second time. 'Sally, my lady, if it please you. I have fetched down all your things and spent the afternoon getting them pressed for you.'

So . . . this was to be her permanent chamber. Her brother had better not return to find her here or he would be enraged. She was supposed to remain out of sight, away from society at all times, and until now she had obeyed his instructions to the letter.

'Thank you, Sally. That will be all. I shall ring if I require you later.'

The appetizing aromas wafting from the tray were making her desperate to start her meal. She lifted the first napkin and stared down in delight. After many years of short rations in the nursery she could hardly believe all this is food was for her.

A tureen of vegetable soup, roast fowl and potatoes, salad leaves and fresh radishes. A veritable feast. Under the second cloth was a dish of strawberries, a jug of cream and a selection of dainty pastries. To drink there was a jug of buttermilk and a jug of fresh lemonade. She wished she could share this with the children, they deserved such culinary treats far more than she.

After two bowls of soup, she found herself unable to tackle anything else. However, she had no intention of letting the tray out of her sight. She would eat her fill during the evening and when she rose in the morning.

The food would keep fresh enough if she covered the tray with a damp cloth. The napkins were ideal for this purpose. She used the jug of boiled water that had been left beside her bed.

Should she leave the tray visible? Would Sally come in and, believing the meal finished with, take the tray away to share amongst her friends? Certainly, in Thorrington Hall the staff ate better than she did. Her room was on the west side of the house, until the sun set it would remain hot. Where should she put her food to keep it fresh?

Under the chest of drawers, if there was not too much dust, would be ideal.

That done, she returned to the privacy of her bed, drawing the hangings around her. If anyone came in, she would seem to be asleep. She had no wish for further conversation with Jane tonight. If Edward was back, she didn't wish to know. That way she could sleep peacefully, believing tomorrow she would be free of him forever.

She clasped her hands in front of her and thanked the Almighty for intervening in her life. Only the hand of God had given her this extraordinary opportunity. All she knew about her prospective husband was that he was wealthy, handsome, a widower and had more than one child. Whether his union had been a happy one she had no idea. His wish to keep their marriage unconsummated could mean he found her so unattractive he could not bear to share his bed with her. On the other hand perhaps he had been so much in love with his first wife the thought of being with another woman was abhorrent.

She giggled. He was a vigorous man; she could not imagine him without female company of some sort. Did he have a mistress? Someone he could not marry, but wished to remain faithful to? She had agreed to be his wife in name only, to love his children and remain in the country, she would not enquire about his private life.

She was used to following orders. Now was not the time to question or to disobey.

5

'Damnit, man! What did she say?'

'Lady Eleanor has agreed to your proposal, my lord. The details I require in order to obtain the marriage licence are written on the back of your missive.'

Alex stuck out his hand and Foster placed the paper in it. She was four and twenty, the middle name was Martha. There was nothing else. She asked no questions, made no demands — just sent the details.

'Did Lady Eleanor send me a message of any sort?'

'Her ladyship said no one must know of your nuptials. I am to bring a curate from Town to perform the ceremony. She intends to remain in her room until everything is ready for the ceremony.'

'Good man. I am glad that is settled. I am not receiving and shall remain in my bed until tomorrow.'

'Very well, my lord. I'll arrange for someone to take my place whilst I'm absent. Would you prefer it if I sent young Sam up from the stables?'

'Sam? Why the devil should I want a groom

56

in my bedchamber?' His head was pounding and he was finding it increasingly difficult to concentrate.

'I thought someone in your employ, who could be relied on not to gossip, would be preferable.'

'Of course; I should have thought of that. Make sure you have sufficient funds to travel post in both directions, and I expect the fee for the licence might well be several guineas.'

Foster collected what he needed and left his master in peace. When the door opened, from the whiff of stable, Sam had come to tend him. Alex required nothing; sleep was the best healer.

★ ★ ★

Eleanor heard the door open softly but remained silent, hidden behind the hangings on her bed. The door closed again and she was left in the darkness; only the moonlight filtering through the shutters lit the chamber. The girl who had been assigned to her could be heard moving around the room before she, too, departed for her bed.

Certain she would not be disturbed again that night, Eleanor pushed back the curtains and scrambled out of bed. Taking the candlestick she carried it to the mantel shelf and deftly used the tinderbox. She moved around the room, lighting them all until she was able to see enough to read. Next, she retrieved the tray and put it triumphantly on the octagonal side table.

Good heavens!

The maid must have been looking for the missing tray. She hoped there would be no repercussions downstairs. How thoughtless of her! She removed the cloths — even the cold soup remained appetizing. Determined to stay up all night if necessary in order to devour every last morsel, she set to with gusto.

Again her appetite failed before she had attempted the desserts. The buttermilk was the most likely to turn rancid overnight so she finished that off before replacing the napkins, freshly dampened, across the remainder of the food. There was no need to secrete the tray under the drawers, no one was going to come in and take it away before the morning.

Having slept for several hours, she was wide awake and restless. The last thing she wanted was to dwell on was what was to take place the following morning. Was she stepping from the frying pan into the fire?

Lord Bentley had shown himself to have a fearsome temper. Had she not seen for herself how he had ripped his sleeves from his jacket in order to . . . ? Why had he done so? Now that she recalled the incident more clearly he had not railed at her, had not been shouting or swearing. In fact, he had made no move to harm her. Only when Ned had attacked him had he seemed angry.

Was it possible that she had misjudged the situation? Had she attacked an innocent man? In which case it made no sense for him to offer to marry her in order to make amends for *his* behaviour.

No, he had regretted his fury and wished to make things right.

She sighed. She could not fathom this at all. What mattered was he had offered her an escape route.

Did he not say in his letter that he had already decided she would suit him as a wife? The incident had only precipitated matters; no doubt he would have spoken to her at a later date. This way her brother would not be able to prevent it. His permission was not legally necessary — she was well past her majority — but Society would have expected Bentley to speak to him first.

No point in repining; she would be better off spending her time selecting something suitable to wear for the ceremony the following day. Taking two candles, she walked into the dressing room and pulled open the doors of the massive closet.

Well, it wouldn't take her long to make a decision; she only possessed six gowns.

Two of these had been turned and re-sewn twice already, two were plain brown and even her brother said she looked hideous in them and one she had ruined with Bentley's gore.

This left her the one smart ensemble she owned, and that was really a misnomer. She fingered the faded silk which remained a pretty pink. Fortunately the waistline was fashionably high, but that was all that could be said to recommend it as a wedding dress. At least this gown possessed silk stockings and slippers to match as well as a gossamer wrap.

Perhaps, if she added a new sash and refurbished the silk roses sewn around the hem and neckline, it would do. Her sewing box had been brought down with her other things. Eagerly she rummaged through, she was certain there was a length of ribbon that would be perfect. Over the years she had become expert at trimming bonnets and such. She was allowed no pin money at all and was entirely dependent on her brother for any purchases she wished to make. However, Jane had often brought her back little gifts of haberdashery which Eleanor treasured and used to embellish the sad garments that were her wardrobe.

The sun was rising before she had completed her task. She hung her dress back in the closet, satisfied she would not look quite such an antidote in the morning. As soon as the girl appeared she would demand a bath and wash her hair; that alone would make her feel more feminine.

Finally tired enough to sleep she scampered into bed, forgetting to extinguish the remaining candles. She was drifting off to sleep when she remembered her dereliction but for the first time since her dear mama died, she ignored this duty. For some strange reason she was now being treated as a true house guest, and no one, this time, would rail at her for such extravagance.

★   ★   ★

Alex took the laudanum the physician had left him and slept dreamlessly through the night. He was roused by the sound of clattering in his dressing room. He must attempt to stand upright. He was not going to be married from his bed, however urgent the matter might be.

His memory had not returned. He still had no recollection of anything past his entry into the wood. Once they were safely married he

61

would demand that Lady Eleanor tell him exactly what had taken place. Fortuitously, this woman fitted his requirements perfectly. He would have been obliged to marry her even if she had been a veritable pea-goose.

'Sam, where the hell are you? I want to get bathed and dressed.'

The erstwhile groom appeared at his side. 'I ain't used to all this paraphernalia, me lord. I never knew it were so complicated to get up if you was a gent.'

Ignoring this inappropriate remark, Alex gave his instructions. 'Send the chambermaid down to arrange for hot water for my bath to be brought. Get her to bring something to eat, and coffee, black.'

'Do you need a hand to get out, sir? It's a right long time since you — '

'Exactly so. Here, let me lean on you; my head's spinning.'

Refreshed, and relieved, Alex practised walking around the bedchamber until he was fairly sure he could remain upright without support. The bath was being filled in his dressing room. He would feel more himself when he was clean and dressed. The tray of food didn't interest him, but he must eat something if he was to get through the day.

Sam heaved him out of the bath. His legs

were as weak as those of a newborn foal. He decided to rest until Foster returned from London. Once his manservant was there to assist him, dressing would take no more than thirty minutes.

Dismissing his temporary assistant, he sank back on to the pillows. The physician had said amnesia was not uncommon after a head injury and that his memory might well be fully restored in time. However, the quack had not committed himself as to when this might happen. He might recall the missing events tomorrow or several months in the future, or never.

He abandoned the notion to question his new bride; better to let her forget all about it, to build bridges and establish trust and friendship between them. As soon as they were married they would leave the abbey and return to Blakely Hall, his ancestral home in Suffolk. This monstrous pile, built in the time of good Queen Bess, desperately needed the loving touch of a woman. Most of it was under holland covers. The children used only the nursery and the few servants he had kept on after Anna's demise rattled about in the east wing.

This left the problem of where to hold the marriage ceremony. He could hardly invite Lady Eleanor into his apartment and he could not go to hers. Perhaps they could marry in the nursery; the nursemaids and Foster could act as witnesses. Although his face was clean, the bandage around his head made him look grotesque. He hoped his fearsome appearance would not make her change her mind.

God's teeth!

How the devil was Foster going to spirit in the curate without it being remarked on by any of the other guests? His man was resourceful; he would no doubt introduce him as a lawyer or some such fustian. The time was a little after ten o'clock, with luck the business would be concluded satisfactorily by noon.

He frowned and regretted it. When he had married Anna, it had taken weeks of negotiation with the lawyers to arrange a satisfactory settlement. All this would have to be organised after the event, rather than before. Whatever money his wife might bring to the union he would have settled on her to do as she wished with. He would also ensure she had sufficient pin money to replace her hideous wardrobe.

Would Sarah approve of his choice? He would not be in this predicament without her interference. He closed his eyes, could see his mistress smiling down at him, her golden curls loose around her shoulders, her full breasts . . .

He stopped. Despite his fearsome headache his groin tightened. How he wished she was with him now. She would enjoy the secrecy, the intrigue of it all. The sooner he got back to London the better.

* * *

Eleanor had been curled up on the window seat, her hair loose around her, allowing the sunshine to dry it, for an hour or more. A second message from Lord Bentley had informed her that the ceremony was to take place at half past eleven, in the *nursery* of all places. Time to get dressed.

Thankfully, she had received no visitors. Jane would take the opportunity of her husband's absence to remain in her chambers. Edward demanded his wife be dressed and ready to do his bidding by nine o'clock each morning.

'Shall I put your hair up for you now, my lady, or do it after you're dressed?'

Reluctantly Eleanor stood up. 'I shall put on my under things, Sally, and then you may do it. I do not wish to crease my gown by sitting in it.'

At ten minutes before the appointed time

she was ready. She did not look exactly pretty, but with her hair freshly washed and arranged in a more becoming style she would do. Her newly refurbished dress gave her confidence; she looked better than she had done for years. Sally had suggested she pad the bodice to give her a more feminine outline but she had declined.

The last thing she wished to do was attract unwanted attention from her future husband. What took place in the bedchamber between a man and his wife was a mystery and she wished it to remain that way. Neither her mama nor Jane appeared to derive any pleasure from it.

'There, my lady, you look grand. I don't reckon anyone will recognize you.'

'Thank you, Sally. I am going up to the nursery to see the children; they must be most concerned about my disappearance.'

Eleanor waited until the girl had gone and then headed for her boudoir. She opened the door to the corridor and peeked around. She had no wish to meet any of the other guests and be delayed. Thankfully, it was still too early for most to be up. She sped across and on to the back stairs that led directly to the nursery floor.

Emerging slightly breathless at the door, she paused and checked her skirt was hanging as it should and then stepped through. She could hear the sound of male voices coming from the schoolroom. Her stomach hollowed. She was tardy; would he be angry with her? It was imperative she made a good impression today of all days.

Her feet dragged, her palms were damp, she hesitated — staring out through the gable end to the driveway that stretched into the distance.

Oh God!

A carriage was approaching at a canter; her brother was returning from Town. There was no time to delay. Unless the ceremony was conducted immediately it would not take place at all.

★　★　★

Alex glanced at his fob watch for the third time. There were still two minutes to the appointed time. The children had been removed and taken to the maze by an under nursery maid. Foster had told him the nursery maid had been delighted on hearing the news of the marriage. He supposed, like everyone else, the servant believed he had no other option having ruined the reputation of her mistress.

No, not her mistress; Thorrington's wife

held that position. Whatever the relationship, clearly Lady Eleanor was much loved by all who knew her. He began to feel more enthusiastic about the forthcoming ceremony. His children would have a mother. They must scarcely remember Anna for they had all been little more than babies when she died.

He would introduce Lady Eleanor to his staff, ensure his estate manager and everyone else within his employ knew she had *carte blanche* in his absence. Then he would depart and leave her to establish herself. After this he would go at once to his lawyers in London and sort out the financial side of things. Whatever else he might be, he was not an ungenerous man.

The nursemaid moved to the door. Lady Eleanor had arrived. He hoped he could remain conscious long enough to say his vows; he was feeling decidedly faint. His eyes blurred. He clutched the back of the chair praying his knees would not buckle beneath him.

He blinked several times and swallowed the bile that rose in his throat. The young woman who stepped into the nursery was a stranger to him. What unfortunate quirk of fate had brought one of the guests up to the nursery at this particular time?

6

Eleanor paused. Why was Lord Bentley staring at her with such dismay? The time was barely two minutes past the appointed hour, surely he was not annoyed? Far too late to turn back. She was committed to this loveless union, for she would never get another chance to escape.

'Lord Bentley, I must apologize for being a little late.' She hesitated, concerned by his unnatural pallor. 'You do not look at all well. Are you sure you wish to proceed?'

His eyes lost their frosty look and he bowed slightly. If his valet had not grasped his elbow he might have pitched forward onto his face. 'I did not recognize you, Lady Eleanor, which is why I appeared confused.' He shook the hand from his arm and turned to the curate who was shifting from foot to foot, his Bible clutched tight to his chest. 'Let us get this done, Lady Eleanor is here now.'

Somehow she stumbled through her vows and before she knew it he was pushing a plain gold band over her knuckle. She was no longer Eleanor Thorrington, but Eleanor Bentley. Her brother could not touch her now. A wave of relief flooded through her. She felt the weight of the past few years lift, and she looked up at her husband, her eyes shining and her mouth curved.

'My lord, you cannot know what this means to me. I shall not let you down. I know you wish to leave here today, but permit me to suggest you return to your chamber. You are not well enough to travel at the moment.'

He appeared bemused by her statement, staring at her for the second time as if he didn't recognize her. He was wandering in his wits; his head injury must be worse than it appeared. 'Foster, we must get him back to bed and send for the physician. I am most concerned for his lordship's well-being.'

'Am I not to have a say in this matter?' Her husband's tone was remarkably firm for someone who looked at death's door. 'I have no intention of returning to bed, my dear, I wish to leave here today. I take it you do not have much baggage?'

'I do not, but I cannot leave without saying my farewells to the children. Could we compromise on this, sir? Will you not agree to lie down for an hour or two? This will allow me sufficient time to make ready.'

She thought he would refuse. His eyes narrowed and he stared at her thoughtfully before answering. 'Very well — two hours, no more. My carriage shall be outside at half past one. I expect you, and whatever belongings you wish to bring, to be in it.'

Foster smiled at her and she knew she had at least one friend. Curtseying gracefully, she nodded. 'Thank you, my lord.' She intended to take his other arm but his valet shook his head and she remained where she was.

Walking slowly, but definitely unaided, Lord Bentley left the schoolroom, followed by his manservant. No sooner had the door closed behind him than she was enveloped in a hug. Unused to such demonstrations of affection, she stiffened instinctively and Betty immediately released her.

'I beg your pardon, Lady Eleanor, but I'm that pleased for you. He's a good man, whatever the circumstances. You'll be better off with him than you are at the moment.'

A slight cough behind them reminded them they were not alone. The curate was waiting for the marriage certificate to be signed by the witnesses.

'This has to be done in front of me, my lady. I cannot leave the premises until Mr. Foster has made his mark as well.'

'I am sure he will return immediately once he has escorted Lord Bentley to his chambers. It will be in order for you to wait up here until he does so. Betty, please send down for refreshments for Mr. Anderson. I am going to arrange for my packing to be done, and then shall go out to the maze and speak to the children. I doubt that I shall see you again, at least not today.'

Eleanor couldn't continue, Betty and Mary were the only friends she had. They had been good to her and she would miss them. She prayed Edward did not vent his spleen on his children when he discovered her defection. He could keep her inheritance. As long as she was out of his reach, that was all she cared about.

'Good luck, my lady, and don't worry about us. We shall manage well enough.'

Eleanor met no one on her on her way downstairs. The tall clock on the landing struck midday. Good heavens! In the space of less than half an hour, she had irrevocably changed her life. She was tied to a complete stranger, had agreed to honour and obey him. What had possessed her to take such an impulsive action?

The noise of someone entering through the front door spiralled up from the vast entrance hall and into the gallery a few yards from where she stood.

Edward.

The thought of meeting him shocked her into movement and she ran to her apartment.

She burst in to find Lady Haverstock and her sister-in-law waiting for her.

★   ★   ★

Somehow Alex found the fortitude to walk unaided to his own chambers. Foster knew better than to offer to assist, but he was aware his man was hovering beside him in case he collapsed. Fortunately, he reached his destination without disgracing himself.

'If I lie down I doubt I shall be able to get up again today. I shall sit quietly in this armchair, Foster, and leave you to get things organized.' He gripped the padded arms of the chair and carefully lowered himself; any sudden movement made his head swim disastrously.

He was seriously concussed. Foolish to think about travelling the fifty miles to his home, but it was imperative to remove his wife from the insidious influence of Thorrington.

Once stationary, he risked opening his eyes again. Foster had vanished; he was alone. He settled back and let his mind drift over the last half hour. What must the poor girl have thought when she entered the room and he'd failed to recognize her? He hoped she had not been offended. He could hardly credit how different she looked this morning. Her gown was elegant, her hair transformed to a lustrous chestnut brown.

After the ceremony when she had smiled up at him, she was another woman entirely. She had looked years younger, as if she was delighted to be his wife. No, it was more than that. She had looked triumphant. Why was that?

He thumped the arms of the chair. Why could he not remember what had taken place the day before?

There was something decidedly havey-cavey about this past twenty four hours. As soon as he was himself again he would make it his business to discover exactly what it was.

★ ★ ★

'Eleanor, where ever have you been? I can see the children at the maze, so you were not with them.'

'Jane, Lady Haverstock, I do hope you have not been waiting here long. I went up to the nursery to speak to the children, but as you so rightly point out they were not there so I stayed to talk to Betty.' She kept her left hand firmly behind her back.

'I do not recollect seeing that gown before and your hair is arranged differently this morning.'

'I am amazed that you do not recognize it, Jane. I have had it this age. I have merely added fresh trimmings from my sewing box.' She smiled at her hostess. 'I'm sure Lady Haverstock would not wish me to appear in my work clothes, not when I am sleeping down here.'

The two ladies exchanged anxious glances. 'We have come to speak to you about your accommodation, my dear.' Jane looked decidedly uncomfortable. Eleanor guessed what was coming next. 'As you are now fully recovered from your unpleasant experience we thought you would not mind returning to your previous chamber. There are unexpected guests arriving later today. I'm sure that you understand, my dear.'

'Of course. I shall pack my belongings immediately. If I could borrow a footman to transport them I should be most grateful, Lady Haverstock.'

'Send the girl when you are ready, Lady Eleanor. You are most gracious, and I apologize for discommoding you in this way.'

The reappearance of her brother had prompted this request. He would be furious if he discovered her mixing with the other guests. The ladies fluttered out and she rang the brass bell to summon the maid.

'Sally, please repack all my belongings in my trunk, but do not have it taken upstairs. I am going out to speak to the children and shall arrange for its removal myself when I return.'

The girl looked disappointed. 'Oh, my lady, what a shame. I doubt you'll have need of me now.'

Eleanor had no maid of her own; would Sally agree to accompany her? 'Are you happy here? If I was able to offer you a position as my abigail, would you take it?'

'I am mostly a maid of all work, my lady, but it has been a right pleasure looking after you. I would be ever so pleased to work for you permanently.'

'In which case, Sally, I'm going to trust you with a secret.' Eleanor held out her left hand. 'I am now Lady Eleanor Bentley. I shall be leaving here in less than two hours. Do you wish to come with me?'

'Lawks a' mussy! Married? I'm right pleased for you, my lady. Of course I will come with you. I shall pack your trunk and then slip upstairs and get my things. Rest assured, no one will hear your news from me. Thank you for giving me this chance. I shan't let you down.'

'I'm sure that you won't. If Lord Thorrington sends word for me to visit him can you lie for me? Tell him I shall come at two o'clock. By then we should be away from here.'

To put on her chip-straw bonnet was the work of moments. Her newly appointed maid fussed over her in a way she was not accustomed to and she found it irksome. The girl meant well, and after all, her duty was to see her mistress was turned out correctly.

She met no one on the stairs or in the vestibule and for that she was grateful. Using the side door, she hurried across the lawn to the maze in which she could hear the four children racing about in excitement. There was no good time to say farewell to her niece and nephews. God knew when she would be allowed to see them again. Leaving them happy was the best she could hope for.

Amanda spotted her first and squealed with delight. 'Aunt Eleanor, we have missed you. Are you coming back to us now?'

'No, darling, I am not. I have come to tell you something very important. Boys, can you come out and join us?'

She led them over to a secluded arbour in which there was a stone seat large enough for the children to be seated. When they were settled, she smiled at them. How could she bear to leave them like this? Who would protect them if she was not there?

'I am sorry that you were obliged to lie yesterday. I had no wish for you to be involved in my crime. I should not have attacked Lord Bentley in that way. I could have killed him.'

'He was so angry, Aunt Eleanor. I could not let him hurt you like Papa does.'

'I know, Ned, you were so brave to rush to my defence. When I saw him shaking you, I acted out of instinct. The branch was within my hand's grasp and I took it without thinking.'

Jonathan spoke up next. '*He* is back. What will happen now?'

'That is what I have to tell you. I am leaving here shortly. I am now Lady Bentley. In future, I am to look after Lord Bentley's children. I shall not be able to live with you.'

Amanda launched herself into her arms, sobbing wildly. The boys, including Ned, joined them on the ground. The children took some time to recover sufficiently for Eleanor to explain as best she could why she had decided to marry a complete stranger.

'You know how things are for me. Your father has made my life intolerable these past few years, and I honestly believe that you will be better off without me.' The wails of protest that greeted this remark told her she still had work to do to convince them she was doing the right thing. 'Children, you must under-stand: without me, your father will not be so

78

angry. For some reason he dislikes me and uses you as an excuse to bully me. Your mother has let things remain as they are because she knows I stand between you and your father. Now she will intervene herself.'

Even as she spoke, she knew all she had done by marrying Bentley was to transfer the problem to Jane's shoulders. Her sister-in-law was not as strong as she was. If Edward treated her as brutally, she would crumble and then the children would have no one to protect them.

The sound of the stable clock striking the half-hour told her she must leave. There was barely time enough to get back to her room and arrange for her trunk to be taken down to the carriage. 'You must be strong. Ned, I am relying on you to take care of your brothers and sister. Once I am established and secure in my position, I shall invite you and your mother to come and stay with me.'

Mary was obliged to prise Peter and Amanda from her legs; Ned and Jonathan stood silently, holding back their tears with difficulty. What had she done? In order to save herself, she had broken the hearts of these dear children. It was too late to repine, they were no longer her responsibility. She must trust Jane and Betty to take care of them now.

Lord Thorrington stared at his wife incredu-lously. 'You did what? You moved Eleanor downstairs where she could be seen by other guests? How many times do I have to explain to you, you stupid woman, that however appall-ing she looks she is still a wealthy heiress and a member of the aristocracy? People have forgotten about her. If she is recognized, some fortune hunter might well persuade her to marry him.'

'I beg your pardon, my lord. Lord Haverstock insisted she was moved down-stairs after she returned covered in blood and so distraught she could not answer a question coherently.'

'That's as may be. At least you have had the sense to move her back.' He turned away, smiling to himself.

This assault on his sister was the best thing that could have happened. She was damaged goods now and no one would want to marry her however enticing her fortune. The lawyers he had been closeted with assured him that as long as she did not marry before her next birthday he could continue to control her trust fund.

Not being able to dip into the capital more often was a damnable nuisance, but the interest was sufficient to keep his family in relative comfort. He had been on a repairing lease these past few months. In October his dividends would be paid, the quarterly rents from his various estates also. Then he would be solvent again.

He scowled. What a pity Bentley had not finished Eleanor off; as her next of kin he would have inherited all her money. Sometimes when she defied him and he was forced to beat her into submission, he had difficulty containing his rage. Her death from natural causes would suit him very well, but he was not a monster. He would not deliberately dispose of her however tempted he was to do so.

'My lord, are you not going to call Lord Bentley out for his temerity? That is what everyone expects.'

Edward spun and his open hand cracked against his wife's cheek, sending her reeling backwards. 'How dare you tell me what to do? I have no interest in what people think or expect. I shall speak to the man and demand an apology. If one is not forthcoming then society will ostracise him. I have no need to put myself outside the law.'

The sound of his wife's muffled sobbing drove him from the room. One thing he would say of his sister — *she* was not so feeble a single slap would reduce her to tears. Eleanor had, it seemed, cracked her attacker on the head. This meant Bentley, according to his snivelling wife, was still incommunicado. The longer the better. He would write him a note, demand an apology, and that could be the end of the matter.

The sound of carriage wheels attracted his attention and he sauntered to the window that overlooked the turning circle at the rear of the house. He did not recognize the carriage. There wasn't an emblem emblazoned on the side, but the equipage was extravagant and must belong to a wealthy man.

He was about to turn away as the vehicle completed its circle and for a moment was parallel to the house. To his astonishment he saw his sister sitting inside, and what looked like Bentley lounging opposite her.

7

As the carriage swung around, Eleanor glanced up at the nursery windows, knowing the children would be there. The row of faces, white blobs against the glass, made her throat thicken and her eyes fill. She blinked. A movement at a window on the first floor caught her attention.

Edward.

She shrank back against the squabs, praying he hadn't seen her. Sally, who was sitting next to her, clutched her hand. Her brother had recognized her. Her husband was slumped on the far side taking up most of the seat. Foster was squeezed into the far corner. At least they would not know their flight had been discovered.

'What is it, my dear? Are you sad to leave the children?'

Her head flew up to meet Bentley's sympathetic gaze. 'Yes, my lord, they were most distressed at my leaving so suddenly . . . ' Her voice trailed away; she could manage no further explanation.

'When the dust has settled, you must invite Lady Thorrington and your niece and nephews to stay at Blakely Hall. It will be good for my ... our children to have playmates.'

She rummaged in her reticule until her fingers grasped her handkerchief. When she had wiped her eyes and blown her nose, she felt ready to ask some important questions. 'If you are feeling well enough to talk, sir, there are some things that I need to know.'

'The names, ages and dispositions of the children?'

'Yes, indeed. I wish to be a good mother to them ... ' She paused, perhaps this was not the time to talk about her duties as a wife.

'Lucy is the oldest. I'm not sure of her age.' He turned to Foster for assistance.

'Miss Lucy is eight, Miss Elizabeth seven and Master Alexander is five, my lord.'

'Thank you. I have spent so little time at Blakely since my first wife died that I have lost contact with them. I am relying on you to supply what I cannot.' He closed his eyes and drifted off to sleep.

Eleanor was horrified at his callousness. When the children had lost their mother so tragically *he* should have supplied the love and stability they needed and not abandoned them to the care of servants. They must have been devastated to be ignored in this way. She would not be surprised to discover they had run wild with no parent to supply firm guidance as well as love.

They were obliged to stay for one night at The Red Lion in Colchester High Street. Foster organized the accommodation and took care of his master. She and Sally ate supper upstairs and were waiting at half past seven the next morning, as instructed, in the vestibule. Today was market day and the noise from the livestock on sale outside made conversation difficult.

The carriage appeared promptly and she decided it would be better to wait inside than stand around being gawped at in the yard. 'Come along, Sally, let us get in. I am sure Lord Bentley and Foster will be with us very soon.'

She had been sitting there a good fifteen minutes before the door opened and Foster almost pushed her husband inside. 'Good gracious! You look decidedly poorly, my lord. Do you think you should be travelling today?'

'We are two hours from my home, madam. If I am to be laid up, I would much prefer to be in comfort.' With that, he collapsed on the seat and closed his eyes. His face had an unnatural waxy hue; she did not like the look of him at all. She leant across and touched his hand. He didn't stir, he was deeply unconscious.

'Foster, I think Lord Bentley is very ill indeed. I do hope there is a good physician to be found when we arrive at Blakely Hall.'

'There is, my lady. I have taken the liberty of sending the groom ahead by post horse. The doctor should be waiting when we arrive.'

The more she knew about her husband's valet the better she liked him. He was more a man of affairs than a mere servant. 'Thank you. I wish we had remained at the abbey until he was well.'

Foster cleared his throat. 'In the circumstances, my lady, it was far better that you left immediately.'

What did he know? Had downstairs gossip revealed the true state of things between herself and her brother? Eleanor hid her face in the brim of her bonnet. She had no wish to discuss her personal life with anyone.

The remainder of the journey was spent in silence, the laboured breathing of her husband the only sound in the closed carriage. She prayed she was not to be made a widow before the day was out. If Bentley died then she was a murderer. Her stomach roiled. What must Foster think of her? His master was at death's door and it was all her fault.

She closed her eyes, trying to make sense of the incomprehensible. Would she be arrested?

Her heinous action had been accepted by her husband, but if he was dead would his family feel the same about the woman who had struck him down? She didn't know if he had any relatives apart from his three children; surely if he had siblings they would have stepped in and offered comfort and a home to his little ones?

Some time later the carriage slowed to travel through a village with well-tended cottages. They trundled past several shops and a hostelry as well as more substantial dwellings and swung sharp right into a winding lane. An ancient church appeared on the left and unexpectedly, across an expanse of lawn bordered by dark yew hedges, she saw what was to be her home. The house was pinnacled, symmetrical, and built from rose red brick. The building was stunning.

A forecourt, flanked by projecting gabled wings, led straight to a bridge defended by stone gargoyles, high above which tapered the fantastic tiers of a clock tower. The vehicle slowed to a walk and halted in front of the house. In order to enter, one was obliged to cross a bridge over a dry moat.

Eleanor could scarcely take in what she was seeing. She could not see the main portal as it was set back some way behind another beast protected arch.

'My lady, do you wish me to remain here and take care of Lord Bentley?'

'Yes, please do so, Foster. I shall go in at once and introduce myself to the children. They must not know that their papa is grievously ill.'

Several footmen appeared and their feet echoed on the bridge. The carriage door was flung open and the steps let down. One of the servants offered her an arm. Shaking her head, she descended unaided. She was pleased to see a tall young man, dressed soberly, stepping forward to greet her. This must be the doctor, it could be no other.

'Lady Bentley, I am Dr Stansted, at your service. I am here to take care of his lordship.'

'Thank you, sir. I am most concerned about his condition; he has been unconscious since we left Colchester. I pray the journey has not proved too much for him.'

'I shall do my best, my lady. Lord Bentley has a strong constitution. If anyone can recover from such a head injury he can.'

She hoped he was correct with his prognosis. She stepped to one side to allow the two men holding a trestle to approach. They were obviously intending to carry the patient back to the house. Despite the parlous situation, her lips twitched at the thought of her husband's reaction should he wake up and find himself so rudely transported.

When things were less fraught she would enjoy exploring the building and its ancient surrounds, but now she must concentrate on the present. Once through the archway, she crossed a cobbled courtyard in order to reach the front door proper. This main portal was dated *1620*.

Goodness!

Blakely Hall was indeed an ancient structure. An august gentleman in black greeted her with a bow.

'You are welcome to Blakely Hall, my lady. I could wish the circumstances were happier. I am Sydney, the butler. Allow me to introduce you to the rest of the staff.'

Instead of a double row of servants waiting to greet her, there was a mere handful. The tall thin woman in navy bombazine was obviously the housekeeper. This lady curtsied, but did not smile. Four footmen and a handful of housemaids were not sufficient to run a house of this size.

She nodded at the staff and paused in front of the housekeeper, keeping her expression haughty as she waited for the woman to introduce herself.

'Jones at your service, my lady. If you will follow me I will conduct you to your apartment.'

'Where are my children? I wish to see them immediately. Show me to the drawing-room. I shall wait there.'

The woman bristled. 'I shall have them fetched right away. The drawing-room is this way, my lady.'

Ignoring the woman, Eleanor turned to speak to Sally who was hovering nervously behind her. 'I rely on you to prepare my chambers. Demand that one of the inside staff assist you if you are not satisfied with their cleanliness.'

A magnificent staircase dominated the great hall but she did not have time to examine it in detail. The room she was taken to faced east, the mullioned windows looking out over the moat and across to a formal parterre garden. The grounds were immaculate, the sheep and deer keeping the grass short. There might be too few inside staff, but Lord Bentley had not cut back on outside men.

Whilst she waited she examined an extraordinary, carved stone chimney piece. She ran her fingers over the angelic figures that held up a coat of arms. She must suppose this was the family crest, she would ask when . . . when she could. Presumably Lord Bentley was safely established in his own apartment and being attended to by the doctor. No doubt Dr Stansted would speak to her before he left.

Eventually the sound of footsteps approaching interrupted her pacing. She had already removed her bonnet and gloves and checked that her hair was neatly arranged. She was still wearing the gown she had been married in. Sally had sponged and pressed it for her and it did not look too creased.

Placing herself in the centre of the room she rubbed her palms on her handkerchief before returning it to her to her reticule. A sharp rap on the door split the silence. She dropped her bag. The double doors were pushed open and a prune-faced woman of indeterminate years, her hair scraped back in the exact same style she herself had adopted until yesterday, all but pushed three silent children through the door.

To Eleanor's astonishment, the nanny did not introduce herself. She merely dipped in a minimal curtsy and retreated, closing the door with a decided snap.

Not good. Not good at all.

'My dears, shall we be seated on the sofa by the window together? I am your new mama. I shall be living here with you in future and intend to devote all my time to making your lives happier.'

The oldest girl, Lucy, her dark hair cruelly

braided, took the hands of the younger children and edged a little closer. The boy, Alexander, was still dressed in frills and flounces, his hair to his shoulders. If she hadn't known his gender she would have thought him a girl. The middle child, Elizabeth, was the image of her father, her eyes flashed with the same fire.

'Lucy, have you eaten your midday meal? I am famished, I was too excited about meeting you all to eat any breakfast. If I ring for refreshments what shall I ask for? Tell me your favourites and they shall be requested.'

The children exchanged disbelieving glances. 'We do not eat in the middle of the day, ma'am. Nanny says it's good for us to do without until teatime.'

'Well, Lucy my dear, I'm in charge of your welfare now. I think children should eat when they are hungry. Now, tell me where is the bell strap hidden?'

Elizabeth ran to the fireplace and pointed to the silken tassel hanging from the ceiling. 'This is it, my lady. Shall I pull it for you?'

'Please, my love, do so at once.' Eleanor reached down and lifted Alexander on to the seat beside her. 'Now, young man, my first task shall be to have suitable garments made up for you. How can you possibly ride a pony dressed like that?'

The boy lost his worried frown and smiled.

'I should like that, Mama. I can't climb trees neither.'

'I should think not, indeed. But that is for later. First, we must decide what we are to order before someone arrives in answer to the summons.'

The butler came himself to answer the bell. 'Can I be of assistance, my lady?'

Excitement rippled along the row of children.

'We require sustenance at once. We would like apple pie and cream, cheese and chutney and fresh bread and butter, plus a selection of whatever cakes have been baked today. Oh, yes, and fresh lemonade to drink. I believe there is a hothouse? Bring also a basket of whatever fruit is available.'

She had expected him to frown but instead his austere expression softened and he almost smiled. 'I shall tell Cook to prepare it straight away, my lady. Do you wish your meal served in the breakfast parlour?'

'Is that a small and friendly room, suitable for family eating?'

He nodded vigorously. 'Yes my lady. I shall have the food sent along immediately.'

'Come, children, you can show me some of the ground floor on the way.'

Lucy lifted down her little brother. 'Which way would you like to go? We can go through the main hall or out that open door there — it leads to a smaller drawing-room and music room.'

'I must learn to find my way about this huge house as soon as possible. Take me in whichever direction you wish. I shall have to memorize them all.'

Elizabeth made the decision for them. 'I want to show Lady Eleanor the piano; it's out of tune, and I would so like to play it one day.'

'And so you shall, I shall teach you myself as soon as the piano tuner has visited.'

The children were desperate for her attention, vying with each other to point out peculiar carvings, family portraits and anything else they thought might be of interest. The pianoforte was indeed sadly out of tune; she doubted it had been played for several years. With all three milling around her talking non-stop, she had difficulty making note of their direction. She doubted she would be able to find her way back to the drawing-room without assistance.

'Here we are — the breakfast parlour. We do not eat here. We have all our meals in the nursery, but I believe that Papa uses it when — ' Lucy stopped mid-sentence. 'Where is he? Didn't he come with you today? You haven't told us when you got

94

married. Have you known him a long time?'

'Too many questions on an empty stomach. I shall answer them as soon as we have eaten.'

She followed her guides into the chamber at the precise moment a trio of maids arrived with laden trays. Cook had surpassed herself; there was enough food to feed ten children and several adults as well.

'Sit down quietly, children, and we shall say grace together. Then we shall help ourselves to what we want. Alexander, I shall serve you for I doubt you can reach the centre of the table.'

Eventually, they were all replete. Eleanor surveyed the mountain of food that remained untouched. 'There's enough here to pack up a picnic tea and take it down to the lake. Who would like to come with me?'

One would have thought the children had never been on a picnic before as they danced around her. Laughing, she waved her hand and called for hush. 'Before we can go out, there are several things I have to do. The first is to speak to Nanny and see if there is anything more suitable for Alexander to change into. Girls, do you have less elaborate garments you could wear?'

'Nanny said we should change into our best to meet you, ma'am. Perhaps she will

95

allow us to put on something we can run around in.'

'Elizabeth, my dear, if I wish you to change then Nanny must find you something to put on. Shall we go upstairs and speak to her?'

She pushed her chair back and walked across to ring the bell. Sydney appeared so promptly he must have been waiting for her call. She explained to him that she wanted the food and the lemonade put into a picnic basket for later. Following him to the door, she spoke quietly so the children could not overhear.

'Sydney, is Dr Stansted still here?'

'Yes, my lady, he is with Mr Foster. Lord Bentley's man was desirous of speaking with you but I said you were not to be interrupted when the children were with you.'

A sick feeling flooded through her. 'I see. I should like a footman to take me to Lord Bentley's apartment. I shall go and speak to Foster immediately.'

The children would have to go up to the nursery ahead of her. If the news was as bad as she feared, they should not hear it until had time to prepare them. It would not do to alarm them prematurely.

8

Edward watched the carriage until it was out of sight. He couldn't begin his enquiries until his rage was under control. Why had Bentley left with the woman he had attempted to assault? It made no sense.

The red mist slowly cleared and his mind began to function normally. Whatever the reason Eleanor had left Bridgeton Abbey was to his advantage. Her reputation had been damaged yesterday but today what was left would have gone entirely. His sister would be a social outcast; even the most determined fortune hunter would shy away from a match with Bentley's leavings.

He smiled. He would leave the matter for a few hours and then demand to see Eleanor. When she failed to appear, he could initiate a search and her disgraceful behaviour would become common knowledge. Tomorrow was soon enough to discover Bentley's whereabouts and reclaim her. His eyes glittered. This time he could thrash her without remorse. Even his soft-hearted wife would have to accept that it was his right and duty to punish someone who had bought the family name into disrepute.

* ★ ★

'You say that Lady Eleanor is nowhere to be found?' The footman nodded and Edward dismissed him with a curt gesture. He turned to his wife, as ever, hovering in the background. 'Madam, go at once to the nursery and question the children and the nursemaids as to Eleanor's whereabouts.'

The twenty minutes he was obliged to kick his heels did nothing to improve his temper. When, eventually, his wife reappeared, he schooled his features to appear ignorant of the news she was about to give him.

'My lord, Eleanor has left with Lord Bentley. He offered her the position of governess to his children and she accepted with alacrity.'

Jane did not appear cowed or agitated by this news. Indeed, she seemed almost pleased.

'Governess? My sister to work as a servant? This will not do. I will not have it.'

'You're too late. They left this morning. I shall have to appoint a governess myself to replace her. The boys leave for school in September so there will be no need to appoint a tutor for them.'

This defiance was too much for his fragile control. He raised his fist but she was too quick for him. In a swirl of skirts, she spun and vanished into her own boudoir and the sound of the bolt being shot echoed around the room. For the first time in the eleven years they had been married, his wife had defied him.

Lady Haverstock, who was strolling on the terrace below with another guest, looked up in shock as he hurled the ornaments from the tables through the open window. He did not care. He would not be gainsaid. His wife and sister would pay for their disobedience.

★   ★   ★

Eleanor smiled at the three children. 'I had meant to tell you: your papa did, of course, return with me. Unfortunately he's feeling a trifle under the weather. The doctor is with him now, and I must go and see what can be done to make him more comfortable.'

Lucy nodded sagely. 'He is often unwell when he visits us. He is obliged to stay in his rooms most of the time.'

'Things shall be different now I am here, my love. Even when your papa is indisposed, or in Town, I shall be here to take care of you.'

This was enough to reassure them. Unbothered by the absence of their father they led her back to the great hall and up the imposing stairs. They continued to the nursery floor and left the footman to guide her to the master suite.

She hesitated; should she knock? The matter was decided for her as a footman thought she was waiting for him to open the door. He did this with a flourish; announcing her to Foster and the doctor as if she was appearing at a ball.

'I apologize for not arriving sooner, but I have only just received your message.'

The young man bowed. 'The news is far better than you might have anticipated, my lady. Lord Bentley has a concussion, but he has regained consciousness and is perfectly lucid. I'm certain there is no permanent damage and a week or so resting in bed will fully restore him.'

Her legs suddenly refused to hold her upright and she swayed. Instantly Dr Stansted moved forward to guide her to the nearest seat. 'Lady Bentley, this news has been a shock to you. Remain still for a few moments until the faintness passes.'

'I am feeling better, thank you. I had come here prepared for the worst. Relief quite over-whelmed me.' She glanced at Foster. 'Do you require my services in the sickroom? I have experience, I have nursed my niece and neph-ews on many occasions these past few years.'

'No, thank you, my lady. I can manage myself. His lordship would be most displeased if I allowed you to do such menial work.'

'In which case, I shall leave him in your capable hands. If he should enquire as to my whereabouts, I am taking the children down to the lake for a picnic this afternoon.'

'Very well, my lady. Have you met Nanny Brooks?' The warning twinkle told her what to expect when she braved this lady's territory.

'I met Nanny Brooks when she delivered the children to me earlier.' She smiled at the physician. 'I must thank you for your assistance, sir. Shall you be returning again today?'

'No, not unless his condition deteriorates. Foster has instructions to send for me should that be the case. However, my lady, I don't anticipate this happening. You mustn't worry unduly. Lord Bentley has a strong constitution; he will be up and about again in no time.'

'In which case I must bid you good day. Foster, I shall call in when I return.'

She almost skipped from the room. All that remained was for her to vanquish the woman who had controlled the lives of the children these past few years. The fact that Brooks had half-starved them gave her the courage to march into the nursery. Her steps were light.

She was not to be named a murderer after all.

Faced with a row of identical doors along a narrow, uncarpeted passageway on the top floor of the house, she had no idea into which one she should make her entrance. She could manage to remain obdurate in the face of whatever opposition she encountered from Nanny Brooks. However, if it took her several attempts to locate the children she rather thought her courage would evaporate.

The only way to be sure was to listen outside. What if someone emerged from one of the other doors and caught her eavesdropping? Her credibility as the children's mother would be destroyed in an instant. Strange, when the children had left her, they were full of vitality and noise — so why could she not hear them?

She walked briskly across to the door in the centre and pushed it open. Three heads turned, but none of the children got up from their chairs or said a word in greeting.

This would not do. They were petrified. What else could be keeping them so still and quiet?

'Brooks, I wish to speak to you. Now.' Her anger added authority to her voice. She remained where she was; what she intended to say to the woman must be spoken in front of the children. Lucy's eyes widened and

Eleanor braced herself.

The woman was behind her; forewarned, she did not stumble forward in shock. 'Lady Bentley, it's customary for the children to be brought to you. I didn't expect to see you in my nursery.'

Slowly she turned to face the nanny who had been mistreating her husband's dear children for the past few years. 'I am most displeased by the way the nursery has been run. You have overstepped your authority. You are a servant here. These rooms do not belong to you, but to my husband.'

The woman looked less confident. 'Lord Bentley gave the children into my care on the sad demise of their sainted mother. He has never had cause to criticise in any way.'

'That's as may be. Things are different now. *I* am the children's mama and their upbringing is entirely under my control.' She raked the nanny from head to toe and found her wanting. 'You are dismissed from my employ. I wish you to leave immediately. I shall *not* be writing a reference.'

'You can't do that. Lord Bentley appointed me. Only he has the right to send me away.'

Eleanor could feel the malevolence pouring over her and for a moment her determination wavered. Then three small bodies pressed against her. She could not falter.

'How dare you speak to me like that? If you're not gone from here by the time I return, I shall have you removed. Do I make myself clear?'

Forcing herself to remain rigid, she stared icily until Nanny Brooks capitulated. Without a further word, the woman ran from the room and could be heard slamming about next door.

'Well, that's one task completed. The second is to find more suitable garments for you all.'

'Our bedroom is next door, my lady. We can show you what we have and you must choose for us.'

'I shall do no such thing, Lucy. You and Elizabeth are quite old enough to dress yourselves; I shall concern myself with finding something for your brother.'

She was rummaging around in his closet when she became aware she was no longer alone. She turned expecting to face another antagonistic nursemaid. Instead two girls stood beaming at her. The taller, a buxom, blonde-haired young woman, of about seventeen or eighteen summers, curtsied.

'My lady, we heard everything. Is that witch really leaving here?'

'Indeed, Brooks will be gone before the day is out. Tell me your names and duties here.'

'I'm Daisy, my lady, and I'm under nursemaid. This here's Rose, she's none too strong in the attic, if you get my meaning. But she's willing and loves the children as much as I do. It's a crying shame what's been happening up here these past four years.'

'That will be enough on *that* subject, Daisy. Can you manage to run the nursery for the moment? The children will spend the greater part of the day with me. I intend to be their teacher.'

Lucy appeared in a plain green dress, her smock more or less on, her face alight with happiness. 'Elizabeth has nothing to wear. Shall I give her something of mine?'

'Yes, my love, do that.' The girl disappeared and Eleanor turned to Daisy once more. 'Go through and undo Miss Lucy's and Miss Elizabeth's plaits. Leave their hair loose; a ribbon will be sufficient to keep it out of their eyes.'

Alexander danced in, waving a garment over his head. 'Mama, look, knickerbocks. And a shirt and things. I found them myself. Can I put them on please?'

'Well done, young man. Quickly, let us dispose of these silly, frilly items and dress you as Alexander. Tomorrow I shall cut off those ridiculous curls.'

The afternoon was a resounding success. Eleanor returned with the children far later than she intended. Alexander was so fatigued she had to carry him, but was wilting under her burden. She couldn't stagger up three flights of stairs to the nursery without dropping him. He was remarkably light for a child of five years, but she was not herself having had no sleep for two nights.

'Allow me, my lady. I can carry Master Alexander up to the nursery for you.'

'Daisy, wherever did you spring from? Yes, please take him.'

Rose had taken charge of the girls. They were holding her hands and eagerly telling her all about their afternoon.

'I shall leave you to put them to bed. They must have a bath tomorrow; it is too late to worry about a little grime tonight.'

'Yes, my lady. What time do you wish them to be up tomorrow?'

'Good heavens! Let them sleep as long as they want. When they have breakfasted and bathed, bring them down to me. I expect I shall be downstairs with the housekeeper.'

As promised, Eleanor went straight to her husband's apartment to enquire how he did. Foster was waiting to speak to her. His serious expression made her stomach lurch.

'Tell me, he is not worse?'

'No, my lady, Lord Bentley is sleeping comfortably. There is something I feel you ought to know. That appalling Brooks woman left, but took the housekeeper with her. They have long been cronies and feathering their own nests and no one was strong enough to stop it.'

'No doubt we shall manage until I can appoint new staff. Unemployment is rife in the countryside, and with the price of corn so high people are starving. I will have no difficulty replacing those that have left, or in appointing the extra servants a house of this size so desperately needs.'

Too much had happened in these past twenty four hours. She supposed it was her duty to go down and arrange for someone to take over the housekeeper's duties but her feet refused to obey her command.

'If you will allow me, my lady, I should be happy to arrange things downstairs.'

'Would you? Foster, I'm in your debt. But you must not leave Lord Bentley unattended.'

'No fear of that, madam. Sam's there now; he seems to enjoy being an inside man instead of a groom.'

'In which case, I shall retire to my apartment. Today has been tiring. I shall see you in the morning. Remember, if Lord Bentley takes a turn for the worse you must rouse me immediately.'

Her apartment was adjacent to her husband's. The rooms were on the south of the house looking down the drive. Her delightful sitting-room was in the turret and one tall mullioned window faced south, the other west. Sally was waiting for her.

'My lady, I have your clothes all sponged and pressed and there's a bath drawn for you in the dressing room.'

'Has it been there long?'

'No, one of the maids came up to tell me you were on your way back. The water's lovely and hot.'

Eleanor could barely keep our eyes open but the thought of relaxing in a hot bath appealed to her. She followed her abigail into her bedchamber, barely noticing the furniture or decorations in her hurry to reach her dressing room.

'What a lovely room. Sally, make sure the communicating door is locked.'

'I heard Mr Foster turning the key soon after his lordship was there.'

Sinking into the rose-scented water Eleanor began to relax. She closed her eyes, barely listening to Sally's chatter until the girl mentioned the departure of the housekeeper and the nanny. 'What was that you said, Sally?'

'Mrs Jones and Nanny Brooks were that angry. They were saying all sorts of dreadful things. I reckon it was all nonsense, my lady. How could those two cause you any harm?'

'They couldn't, of course. Lord Bentley will be back on his feet by the end of the week and I'm sure will deal with the matter himself.'

★   ★   ★

At Bridgeton Abbey, Edward had regained control and ceased hurling missiles through the window. Lady Haverstock and her friend had long since vanished, no doubt to complain about his loss of temper. To have been defied by first a sister and then a wife was almost too much for a man to bear.

How did the information that Eleanor had not run away with Bentley but was in his employ change things?

His shoulders began to unknot. In the eyes of Society, it would make no difference why she had gone. She had left unchaperoned. He would help the rumours on their way, and within the week she would be received nowhere.

He scowled. Not having Eleanor in his

household to take care of the children was a dam' nuisance but at least the spectre of her marrying and her husband demanding her inheritance had gone forever. He needed a drink. His silver hip flask was empty and the decanter on the sideboard was no longer filled each morning.

He supposed he must apologize for scaring his hostess. He would find her and smooth matters over and then seek masculine company in the billiard room. Where would the ladies be at this time? He glanced at the mantel clock. They would be taking tea somewhere; whilst the weather was so clement they had been gathering under an oak tree on the far side of the abbey. He would try there first. As he was descending the stairs female voices drifted up to him from the hall below.

'It is so romantic! Lady Eleanor's run away to be governess for a handsome lord. She was always such a pretty girl in her youth. Away from her brother's household, she will blossom once again.'

He waited to hear what the response would be.

'I am sure she will, my dear, and then that poor man will fall in love with her and there will be a happy ending for them both. She will become the second wife of Lord Bentley.'

Marry him? Surely not? The man had attempted to despoil her, so why . . .

His head began to pound. Bentley was an honourable man; he would wish to put matters right. What better than to have Eleanor under his roof where he could charm her into agreeing to become his wife?

Never! He would not let this happen. He would kill his sister before he let anyone get their hands on her trust fund.

9

Eleanor was unable to see her husband. Twice a day she visited his apartment and spoke to his manservant, each time to be reassured that he was recovering well. Dr Stansted made a point of seeking her out on one occasion to say Bentley would be allowed to rise from his bed the following day.

She had been alone for four days. The time had been spent exploring the house and grounds; the more she got to know Blakely Hall, the better she liked it. All three children were adorable and she loved them already. However, her happiness was tainted by the fact that the welfare of Bentley's children had been at the expense of her niece and nephews.

Despite the loss of the housekeeper everything was running smoothly although most of the house remained under holland covers. The nursery floor and the two apartments occupied by herself and her husband were in use upstairs, and the drawing-room and small dining-room downstairs. Until they had more staff, it would be impossible to bring the other rooms into use.

Foster had this matter in hand. Sydney, the butler, had a niece ideally suited for the housekeeper's position. The woman, a Mrs. Nayland, was due to arrive later that day.

Although Bentley had told her she was to have free rein in the house, she was reluctant to change things whilst he was indisposed. Sydney had temporarily taken over the duties of the housekeeper; thankfully the remaining members of staff were happy the two pernicious women had left.

Her priority was to replenish the children's wardrobe. Most of the clothes they had were either unsuitable or too small. Apparently, Brooks had been pocketing the money allocated for this purpose. The village seamstress was busy making their new clothes. When these were finished, she would commission a selection of gowns for herself. Her pink silk was the only garment suitable for somewhere as grand as her new home. Sally discovered several trunks of clothes hidden away at the back of the enormous closet in the dressing room.

'Look, my lady, I'm sure between us we could alter these to fit. They aren't the latest fashion, but it would be possible to bring them up to date.'

'I don't know, Sally. These garments must have belonged to Lord Bentley's first wife. I don't think I should use them without his permission.'

Sally was about to close the trunk when Eleanor reconsidered. 'However, in my experience, to gentlemen one outfit is very much like another. If we raise the waist line, and widen the skirt, add a few frills and furbelows, I doubt these would be recognizable to anyone.'

The two trunks were dragged out and the contents spilled in a kaleidoscope of colour across the *chaise-longue* and carpet. There were silks, muslins and Indian cottons in every shade imaginable. Lady Bentley must have been a free spirit to wear such flamboyant colours. Gossip from below stairs told Eleanor that the first Lady Bentley had been the love of his life. She found it difficult to imagine Bentley in love.

Sally held up a particularly pretty muslin that had a matching shawl and spencer. 'My lady, if I use the shawl, I can insert it into the skirt to make it wider. I can unpick the jacket to add a rouleau around the hem.' She pointed to the fashion plate in *La Belle Assemble*.

Eleanor picked up the periodical and looked more closely. The magazine should rightfully have been returned to her sister-in-law, but she was glad she had forgotten to do so.

'Let me look. I think the gown could be altered and look just like this picture. It will then be unrecognizable.' Appearing in a dead woman's garments might be considered inappropriate by the staff, but more importantly, by her husband.

'I shall get on to it right away, my lady. I was only taken on by Lady Haverstock because of my skills with the needle. I spent half my time at Bridgeton Abbey doing mending, thank goodness. Scrubbing floors was hard work.'

Eleanor rummaged through the clothes and removed the ones which needed the least alteration. She selected two afternoon dresses, a riding habit, a promenade dress, and an evening gown. One of them must be tried on before Sally began her alterations.

She selected the Indian cotton. The gown was the right length but hung disastrously at both front and back.

'Oh dear, Sally, I am far too thin to wear these gowns.'

'That makes no never mind, my lady. I can take them in. Mind, I won't cut out all the slack, we might need to let them out again with all this good food we're being served. I'm sure you will soon . . . ' Her voice trailed away.

'I know — I do need to gain weight.

However, my appetite has not yet returned. No doubt, when the good Lord is ready, I shall regain my normal shape. You must do the best you can to make these fit.'

Leaving Sally to begin the sewing, Eleanor made her way to the Long Gallery, where the library was situated; she had asked the children to meet her there after breakfast. They had never had the opportunity to go in and look at the thousands of leather bound books. This room stretched the width of the house, one side being lined with bookshelves, the other with windows overlooking the drive. She had asked the two footmen to dust the shelves and remove the holland covers from the furniture so that she could take her charges in.

'Mama, I didn't know there were so many books in the whole world,' Lucy exclaimed.

'I can't reach all the way up, and Alexander will have to take books from the bottom shelf.'

'That's very true, Elizabeth. Shall we start at this end, by the door?'

The children returned to the nursery with several books, eager to show their trophies to the nursemaids. Eleanor had found an illustrated journal, written by an ancestor of Lord Bentley. The more she knew about her husband the better. According to the latest

116

report, he would be rising from his sick bed any day now.

The children were transformed, Alexander especially so. With his hair cut short and dressed as a boy, she doubted his father would recognize him. She hoped her new wardrobe would have a similar effect.

A few days later the Indian cotton dress was ready; Sally had done an excellent job for it fitted perfectly. Eleanor gazed at her reflection.'

'I cannot believe what a difference a fresh gown makes, Sally. I scarcely know myself as the same person who arrived here a short while ago.'

'You look a picture, my lady. And with your hair arranged in that new fashion, you look just like the lady in the picture. I reckon all the exercise you're getting out in the park with the children is doing you good.'

Eleanor smiled. 'Is that a gentle reminder, Sally, that a lady should use a parasol or wear a bonnet?'

'I reckon you should wear one, my lady. You will be brown as a berry if the weather continues like this for much longer.'

'If I had more than this one bonnet, then no doubt I would wear it more often. But I love to feel the sun on my head and to be able to walk freely and hear the children laughing.

As I have no intention of being seen anywhere but here, I hardly think it matters if I'm not fashionably pale.'

★ ★ ★

'I'm getting up, Foster. I have languished in my bed long enough. I don't give a damn what the doctor said. I'm quite capable of being on my feet.'

'Very well, my lord. Perhaps you could put on your dressing gown? The windows are open; you could sit in an armchair and look out on to the park.'

Alex had been going to refuse, to insist that he dressed, but when he sat up his head swam. He would be wise to take things slowly. 'How long have I been unwell?'

'A week tomorrow, my lord.'

Too long. His intention to leave Lady Bentley to get on with it and return to the arms of his mistress were in disarray. God knows what Sarah would be thinking. In the eighteen months since they had first come together he had never been away from her so long.

'I need to write a letter. Bring me my escritoire once I am settled next door.'

Foster draped a robe around his shoulders and Alex walked without assistance into his sitting room. He was drawn towards the window; the sound of children laughing and a woman talking to them, made him curious. He couldn't remember hearing such a thing at Blakely since his darling Anna died.

He stopped at the window, grasping the mullions for support. He was hallucinating. Going down the steps that led from the terrace was his beloved, their three children gambolling around her skirts as happy as puppies in the sunshine.

He closed his eyes and grief overwhelmed him. To be reminded so cruelly of his loss was unbearable. The tallest child, Lucy he supposed, called out to the woman.

'Mama, are we really to play cricket?'

A laughing reply followed this query. 'Indeed we are, my love. Look, set out on the grass are two wickets, ball and a bat. It will be a makeshift game with only four of us, but fun nonetheless.'

Alex brushed away his tears; he was not going mad after all. The woman was not Anna, but someone masquerading as her, dressed in a gown he had chosen himself. He felt a touch on his arm. 'Foster, who is that impostor?'

'That's your wife, my Lord. Lady *Eleanor* Bentley.'

'Devil take it! Why is the wretched woman

wearing my dead wife's clothes? Has she none of her own?'

'No, my lord, she has not. She and her maid servant have altered several gowns to fit.'

Alex's mouth filled with bile. He turned away in disgust. He had made the most horrendous mistake. He should never have married Eleanor. There should not be a second Lady Bentley, however desperate the needs of his children. Seeing her wearing Anna's favourite gown, surrounded by *her* children, and being called *mama* in her stead was too much.

'I don't care if she has nothing else to wear. Send for the seamstress from the village; she must get new garments made. Those she has stolen are to be removed from her possession immediately. Do I make myself clear?'

For the first time in their long acquaintance his man stared at him with dislike. 'I shall have it done, my lord. You do not look at all well. Do you wish to return to your bedchamber?'

Alex gestured him away. 'No, I shall remain here. Get rid of those things before she returns to her apartment. Burn them; it's what I should have done four years ago.'

He collapsed into the nearest armchair disgusted with himself. He was behaving appallingly, the poor girl could not possibly have known her actions would upset him. But it would not do. He could not bear to see anyone else in Anna's clothes.

* * *

'I am quite exhausted, children. I think it is high time we went in. Run upstairs to the nursery. Betty will be waiting for you. I shall come up later to read you a story.'

She watched them scamper away, laughing and chattering. She could hardly credit how much they had changed in the week she had been with them. Although *she* had not regained her appetite, the children were eating well and were no longer subdued.

Her eyes filled. What were her niece and nephews doing without her? Ned and Jonathan would be going away to school next month, but Peter and Amanda would need a governess. Would Jane employ one or take over their education herself?

As always at this time of day, she went to speak to Foster. She walked straight in to Bentley's parlour. The room was not empty as she expected. She recoiled at the look of disgust on her husband's face.

'I beg your pardon, my lord. I had no idea you were in here. I called to speak to Foster.'

He did not rise from his chair, made no move to greet her. A weight settled in her stomach; he was obviously regretting his decision to marry her.

'You are wearing my wife's gown. I do not wish to see you in it again. I am not receiving visitors today.' His voice was curt. He spoke to her as if she were a stranger, and one that he cordially disliked.

She backed out. Her fingers slipped on the handle as she attempted to close the door. He had recognized her dress, he was sickened at her wearing it. She should have known better, should have waited until the seamstress had made her something new.

She would remove it immediately and put on the faded pink gown. This had been washed and pressed and would do until she had others ready. Sally greeted her with a blotchy face and red eyes.

'Oh, my lady, his lordship's sent for the trunks and everything has been taken away; even the items we've altered, and the ones we were about to change. They're to be burnt.'

'It's not your fault, Sally. I should have known better. Quickly, help me remove this, and then send it down to join the rest. I shall wear what I have; that way I will not cause offence to anyone.'

She ignored the supper tray brought up later. She had been upstairs to read the children their story and left them happily snuggled down in bed. They were unaware anything untoward had happened. She had become an expert at dissembling to children over the past few years.

The letter for her niece and nephews was ready to send. She had addressed it to Prudence Smith, the vicar's daughter. This way her brother could not confiscate it before it reached the children. She would ask Lord Bentley if he would frank it when he was speaking to her again.

As she was replacing a stopper in the ink bottle there was a soft knock on the door. 'Come in,' she called. Putting down her pen, she turned to face her unexpected visitor. It would be Foster; no one else would venture up here so late in the day.

Her stomach lurched. Her husband stood there, immaculately dressed, his cravat a snowy waterfall at his neck. He was a different man from the one who had spoken to her so harshly an hour or so ago. She scrambled to her feet and curtsied.

'My dear, you do not need to curtsy to me. I have come to most humbly beg your pardon for my appalling rudeness. There are things we need to talk about, things I should have told you that would have avoided heartache for both of us.'

'You have had nothing to apologize for, my

lord. It was my stupidity. I should never have — '

He was still standing framed in the doorway. 'May I come in, my dear? I've no wish to intrude, I shall fully understand if you don't wish to speak to me.'

Flushing painfully at her unintentional incivility, she gestured for him to enter. 'I'm pleased to see you up and about. Now that the stitches are removed and the bruising beginning to fade, you are almost restored.'

He took the seat she'd pointed to, flicking aside his coat tails. 'Now, the first thing I must say is that this contretemps is *not* your fault. You could have had no idea seeing you in my wife's clothes would upset me. I had thought myself recovered from the grief of her death, but I find it still as raw today as four years ago. That is not your fault either, but mine. From now on I shall try and put it behind me, for your sake and for my children.'

'Please say no more on this subject, sir. I was thoughtless. I shall instruct the seamstress to make me new garments when she has finished replenishing the children's wardrobe.'

'There's no need to do that, my dear. I have sent a note to London; a friend of mine understands these things. A suitable woman and her assistants will come here posthaste. I shall not have you dressed by any village woman.'

'Thank you, my lord. There are several things I wish to discuss with you. The first is that I've dismissed Nanny Brooks and the housekeeper, Jones, decided to leave with her.'

'Foster told me. I should have done so myself long ago. I have been a delinquent parent. I can already see the difference in the house and the children since your arrival. Blakely is your domain; you shall do as you please here. You have my permission to redecorate and refurbish. I don't intend to spend . . . ' He stopped as if embarrassed.

'I understand, my lord. If the children can see you periodically, they will be content. Perhaps you could ensure you are here on their name days, and for the festive season?'

He cleared his throat and ran his finger round his neck cloth as if it had become uncomfortably tight. 'Exactly. To tell you the truth, I've no idea when they celebrate their birthdays. Once supplied with that information I shall make it my business to be here with them. There's something that you need to know, my dear. I have no recollection of what happened last week, when I behaved so appallingly to you. I can't imagine what possessed me, I'm not usually a man of such low morals.'

She stared at him, not sure what he was talking about. 'Low morals?'

'I tried to force myself upon you, Foster told me what happened. My appalling behaviour was the reason I offered for you. This was the least I could do.'

The blood drained from her face.

Good God! He thought he had molested her. That explained why Jane and Lady Haverstock had treated her with such gentleness. He had no idea she had only knocked him to the ground because he was shaking Ned. He had married her because he thought he had ruined her reputation — whilst she thought he married her in order to save her from retribution.

'My dear, you're unwell. I'm a brute to remind you. My behaviour must have been reprehensible indeed if the very thought of it so upsets you.'

He was so close she could smell the lemon soap he used to shave. Her voice failed her. There was nothing she could say. She could never tell him he had married her unnecessarily. If he knew her secret, he would repudiate her and send her back to her brother. When he recovered his memory, she would most certainly get her comeuppance.

She must enjoy every moment of what little time remained of her stay at Blakely Hall.

10

The next day Eleanor decided to visit the nursery before breakfast. By remaining with the children, she would not be obliged to talk to her husband. How could she have got herself in such a situation? If she had realized he was labouring under a misapprehension, however desperate her circumstances, she would never have agreed to marry him.

As it was to be a union in name only, should she confess the whole and let him arrange to have the marriage dissolved?

The children as always, were overjoyed to see her. They already considered her their mama. This made things even more difficult. If she revealed her secret she would deprive the children of her presence. Already she loved them — would it not be better to put their wishes first?

'Come along, everyone. I thought we could take a picnic down to the lake and spend the day there together having fun. That's why you're wearing your oldest clothes.' Lucy's eyes widened and she clutched Eleanor's hand. 'What is it, sweetheart?'

'Good morning, my dear, good morning,

children. Did I just hear the mention of a picnic?'

'Papa, can you come? Please come with us.' Alexander rushed across and flung himself into his father's arms.

The girls seemed less sure; this would not do. Whilst she was still here one thing she could do was re-establish the connection between Bentley and his children. Gently she pushed the two girls forward and he held out his other arm. For a moment they hesitated and then threw themselves at him with as much enthusiasm as their brother. All three clamoured to be heard.

'Children, do be careful! Your papa has been very poorly. It would not do to — '

He smiled. 'I'm perfectly well, thank you, my dear. As you can see the stitches are gone.'

The mention of stitches distracted the children from their demands that he accompany them on their picnic. He sat down in the window seat with Alexander on his lap and his daughters on either side of him. He flicked back his hair to show them the pink scar.

She studied him closely. How was it possible a man as sick as he was two days ago could now be up and about looking so robust? Apart from being a little paler and thinner about the face, he looked much as he did when she'd first met him. Good grief! Can that have only been ten days ago? It felt like a lifetime. So much had changed.

He glanced up, caught her eye and grinned. Something strange happened to her insides. She must not allow herself to become emotionally entangled with this charming, charismatic man. 'Well, my lord, are you to accompany us or not?'

'Definitely. I well remember the last time we were with children by the lake. I sincerely hope I do not have to do take a swim fully dressed today.'

'Tell us, Mama, why did Papa go in the water in his clothes?'

Laughing, she told the story and Lucy stared pleadingly up at him. 'Papa, can *we* play cricket with you like we played with Mama the other day?'

'Of course you can, sweetheart. Why don't you go and fetch what we need whilst I speak to your mama?'

This was the last thing she wanted. 'If you are to accompany us, my lord, I must speak to Cook about increasing the size of the picnic.'

Somehow he was between her and the exit. 'I wish you to call me by my given name, no more formality. You are my wife and I wish us to be friends.'

She swallowed nervously. 'If you insist, sir . . . Alex, but that will be difficult for me. Even my sister-in-law does not call my brother by his name.'

'Eleanor is a lovely name and suits you, my dear.' The children rushed back, waving the cricket equipment triumphantly. 'Ah! Well done, you three. Let's set out on our expedition.'

Alexander tugged at his coat-tails. 'Papa, you shall get your smart clothes ruined sitting on the grass.'

He ruffled the little boy's hair. 'Quite correct, young man, I shall go at once and put on something my valet will not mind me spoiling.' He winked at her and vanished.

Her pulse gradually returned to normal. 'I have asked for the picnic to be brought out to us, along with something to sit on. Your papa will be changed in a trice. Shall we set off? His legs are so much longer than ours, he will soon catch us up.'

★ ★ ★

Alex wanted to turn somersaults but refrained. How could he have remained aloof from his delightful children for so many years? He was a selfish father. Anna would have been ashamed of him. Wallowing in

130

self-pity and refusing to engage with his offspring was something he would regret for the rest of his life.

He bounded up the stairs to his apartment. From now on things would be different. He'd been given a second chance and he wasn't going to throw it away.

'Foster, where the devil are you? Have I any old clothes suitable for boating and picnicking by the lake?'

His manservant appeared instantly. 'I can find something, my lord. Are you sure you are up to it?'

'Damn it, man, I'll not be mollycoddled. I wish to spend time with my wife and children and what better way than larking about by the water?'

Ten minutes later he was striding after his family. His spirits soared as he watched the children gambolling around Eleanor's skirts. For the first time in many years he felt optimistic; if he could not have love in his marriage, then friendship and affection would do. To see his little ones so happy in her company after so short a time was truly remarkable.

His decision to marry her had been precipitate, but he had made the right choice. She was everything a mother should be: kind, honest and loving.

Increasing his pace, he hailed the group. 'Am I suitably attired? Will I pass muster and be allowed to sit on the grass?'

★ ★ ★

Eleanor glanced over her shoulder at his call. 'Good heavens! Alex, you look like a gardener. Wherever did you find that rig?'

'Foster unearthed it; I feel quite liberated dressed as I am.' He scooped up his son and swung him round. 'I believe, my boy, that I might even take a swim later on.'

Lucy and Elizabeth exchanged anxious glances. 'I don't think Papa should have come out without a coat or neck cloth, and to have his sleeves rolled up . . . Mama, what will the servants think?'

'Girls, your papa can do as he pleases; after all he is lord and master here. If he cares not for the opinion of others, then neither should you. I am wearing an ancient gown, and the brim is coming away on my bonnet.'

Lucy nodded. 'But it's different for you. You do not go about in Society like Papa.'

Smiling, Eleanor hugged the girls. 'Quite right, my love. Look, our spot has already been chosen for us in the shade of the boathouse.'

The three children raced ahead, leaving her

to walk with Alex. A child's chance remark had reminded her that she was a plain moth to his bright butterfly.

'Good God! I thought we were coming on a picnic, Eleanor.'

'I asked for some rugs to sit on, that was all.' Her amusement bubbled up and she could not prevent her giggles from escaping. 'I cannot imagine why they have set up a table and chairs with damask napery and cutlery. There's no sign of a picnic basket. Do you think footmen are going to march across here carrying the food on trays?'

'I sincerely hope not. Do you think if I wave frantically someone will notice and send out to see what we want?'

'Perhaps a flag made from a napkin would be more visible.'

'Excellent, it will seem like we're surrendering.'

She watched his antics, finding him all but irresistible when he was like this. The children joined him in his tomfoolery and they pranced about like dancers around a maypole, waving the white squares above their heads. Whoever saw them would think they had run mad.

'Alex, you may stop now. A positive cavalcade is rushing across the park.'

'In which case, my dear, I shall leave you to

arrange things as you wish. We shall go and see if the punt is usable.'

★ ★ ★

By mid-afternoon they were all wet and dirty and ready to return. Alex was stretched out in the bottom of the punt. The children believed he was dozing; Eleanor was not so sanguine.

'I think it's time we went back to the house, children. I want you to return to the house and ask Mr Foster to bring a dry shirt and jacket for your papa. It's not good for him to be so wet. I shall remain here and tidy up.'

Lucy took the hands of her siblings. 'We can do that, Mama. We've had such fun. I do hope you and Papa will take us on another picnic soon.'

'We shall, my dear, when we have both recovered from today. Good, I can see Daisy coming out to fetch you. Hurry up and meet her then you can give *her* the message. I shall come up after nursery tea to read you a story.'

As soon as they had gone, she hurried to the water's edge. 'Alex? Alex, you must come out of there, it's time to return.' There was no response. Did his face look paler than before? Was he unconscious and not sleeping? If she bathed his face with water it might revive

134

him. She viewed the boat with trepidation; she had avoided getting into it as she had no liking for the water.

She would try one last time to rouse him, if that failed she had no choice, she must intervene herself. 'Alex, wake up. I cannot stand about here all day waiting for you.' Still his eyes remained closed.

Perhaps if she pulled the boat in closer to the bank she could lean in and bathe his face without the necessity of getting into the punt herself. With a napkin in one hand, she knelt and stretched out to grab the edge of the boat. The punt rocked alarmingly, she lost her balance and with a despairing cry fell headlong into the water.

The weight of her skirts was dragging her down. The water wasn't deep. She must not panic. She straightened. Her head cracked on the bottom of the punt. The shock made her release the last of her breath and her lungs filled with water.

★   ★   ★

Alex heard the children leave. Eleanor was calling him, but he was too fatigued to answer. He should not have played that last game of cricket, but the children had been so appealing it had been impossible to refuse.

135

He must gather his remaining strength and get himself out of this damned boat and back on dry land.

Suddenly he was tipped sideways and a deluge of cold water covered him. Coughing and spluttering, he sat up and for a moment was not sure what had happened.

God's teeth! Eleanor has tumbled in.

He rolled over the side and, taking a deep breath, dropped beneath the water.

He could see nothing. There were too many reeds and rushes. He must search blind.

Where the hell was she? Why doesn't she stand up?

Groping forward on his knees, his heart pounding, his chest bursting, his fingers found what he was seeking. Grabbing two handfuls of material, he dragged her from under the boat. With one arm around her shoulders, he stood up.

Her head flopped against his shoulder, her eyes were closed and her lips tinged with blue.

A tight band constricted his breathing.

Please God, not again, not when I've just begun to feel my life is improving.

Pounding feet behind him made him look over his shoulder. Foster arrived at his side and all but snatched his burden. 'Here, my lord, place her ladyship over your knee. We must thump her back to restore her circulation and empty the water from her lungs.'

Alex flung her across his knee and did as he was bid. How long could she remain comatose before she was too far gone to be revived? He felt a slight movement beneath his fingers and then she cast up her accounts on the grass.

'Eleanor, thank the good Lord. I thought you'd drowned for sure. Here, my dear, allow me to help you sit up.'

★ ★ ★

Someone was supporting her as she retched. When she had done she was gently cradled in strong arms. Her chest hurt, her eyes were stinging and she had a decided headache, but she was alive. She opened her eyes to find Alex gazing down at her, his face as white as chalk. He was as wet as she. He must have dived in to fish her out.

'I owe you my life. I fell in and when I tried to stand I cracked my head on the bottom of the punt. I can remember nothing after that.'

His lopsided grin warmed her. 'What in God's name were you doing? How did you come to tumble in?' She shivered. Despite the warmth of the afternoon sun, she was cold.

Immediately he snatched up a picnic rug and enveloped her in it. 'Tell me later, my dear. I must get you inside where you can be taken care of.'

In one fluid movement he straightened, keeping her firmly in his arms.

'I can walk, my lord. Please put me down at once. I have no wish to be carried back like a child.' In fact there was nothing she would have liked more than to remain safely in his hold, but he was in no fit state to be carrying her around.

'Very well, Eleanor. You may walk but I shall keep my arm around your waist just in case you feel faint. Good God, woman, you almost drowned! You're entitled to be carried back to the house after such a dreadful experience.' He placed her on the grass and her knees buckled. She collapsed in a wet heap at his feet.

Foster knelt beside her. 'If I might suggest a compromise, my lord. Allow me to carry Lady Bentley whilst you walk alongside.'

Apparently, she was to have no say in the matter. She was to be handed from one to the other like an unwanted parcel.

Not if she could help it.

'If you could give me your arm, Mr Foster, I would much prefer to walk.'

'You'll do no such thing. Either Foster

138

carries you or I do.' For the second time she was hoisted skywards, but on this occasion it was not her husband but his valet who held her aloft.

Long before they reached the terrace, a small army of anxious retainers rushed out to meet them. She was relieved to be safely in her own chamber with only Sally to attend her.

'My lady, what a to-do! You could have been drowned.'

'But I wasn't, and I don't wish the children to be alarmed. They have only just recovered from the fright Lord Bentley gave them on his arrival.'

Sally curtsied. 'Your bath is drawn, my lady. Let me remove your wet garments; you're shivering.'

Once she was tucked up in bed, warm and dry and her teeth no longer chattering, she was able to review what had happened. Alex had been all but swooning in the bottom of the punt yet somehow he had found the strength to rescue her. He was indeed a remarkable man, which made it even worse that she was lying to him. Tomorrow she would tell him the whole. She would offer to leave if that's what he wished.

As she dozed she thought she heard his voice outside her chamber, then all was quiet.

She must have been mistaken. On the verge of slumber, a gentle finger traced the outline of her mouth. Shocked, her eyes flew open.

'So, my love, you are not asleep as your girl told me. I sent her to reassure the children and slipped in here in her absence. Now, are you well enough to tell me what happened?'

She pushed herself upright. She could hardly object to him being in her bedroom; after all, they *were* man and wife. She wished she had insisted that Sally braid her hair for it was most disconcerting having it floating around her shoulders.

'I thought you had swooned. I was leaning in to bathe your face, but unfortunately the boat moved. Before I could regain my balance, I was in the lake.'

He stared at her as if she were a simpleton. 'You leant on the side of the boat?'

'I just said that I did.'

His eyes were laughing down at her. 'Didn't you realize the boat would move? Why didn't you drag it to the side before you attempted your rescue mission?'

This was too much. Had she not just told him exactly what happened? Her head ached abominably.

'My lord, this conversation is becoming tedious. I have no experience with boats and avoid all forms of water apart from that which I find in my bath. I apologize for my ignorance and promise not to offer you my assistance in future.'

His expression changed. He sat back, no longer friendly. 'I beg your pardon for intruding, my lady. I thought we had become good friends today. I was obviously mistaken.'

The door closed behind him and she wished her words back. They had been getting on so well and now she had offended him by her sharpness. How could she reveal her secret when they were at odds? She would make up for her rudeness and work hard to restore matters between them. When the time was right she would tell him everything.

But the days passed and she was too contented to ruin everything by telling him her secret.

11

Alex had not thought he could feel this relaxed at his country home. He glanced over the newspaper that had arrived that morning. Eleanor was, as usual, scribbling away at her desk. She was his *wife*. These past weeks he had spent with her had made him realize it was possible to enjoy another woman's company.

She looked up and smiled at him. With a resigned sigh he folded his newspaper and gazed expectantly at her.

'My lord, I was wondering what sort of party we should organize for Lucy's ninth anniversary at the end of next week.'

'Good God! I had no idea her birthday was so soon. I shall leave the matter in your capable hands, my dear. I have no idea what children of any age wish to do on their name day.'

She frowned slightly, staring at him, her huge brown eyes demanding he take more interest. 'My lord, we agreed when we spoke three weeks ago that you would be here to celebrate with your children. This does not mean just appearing at the party. You are required to have some involvement.'

He tossed his newspaper to one side, admitting defeat. 'Very well, what do you want me to do? I'll not wear a silly hat or play childish games, but anything else I shall reluctantly agree to.'

'I had thought we could invite the village children and their parents. We could have a series of sporting events for the children; perhaps a tug-of-war, a race or two, and any other activities Lucy might suggest.'

'I shall not be required to take part in any of these things?' She looked too innocent. She was preparing to spring a trap on him, he was certain of it. He sat forward, fixing her with what he hoped was a forceful stare. 'I must have your word I shall not be required to do anything ridiculous. I shall be most displeased if I find I have been misled in this matter.'

Her eyes widened. 'I give you my solemn word, sir, you shall be adjudicator and hand out the prizes at the end. I believe that could be considered as a suitably serious role for the Lord of the Manor.'

'Very well, go ahead and organize things as you see fit. But I don't think it wise to ask the villagers, could not the staff join in instead?'

She stared at him as if he was a simpleton. 'The whole point, my lord, is that our children have *other* children to race with. I hardly think they would enjoy being pitted against the staff.'

Almost five years had passed since Anna had invited the villagers and their families to celebrate Alexander's birth. How could he endure a similar event without her by his side? His pleasure in the moment evaporated like water on a summer's day.

'I shall leave arrangements to you. The new housekeeper appears to be as efficient as her uncle. Get her and Foster to assist you. The estate manager, Davies, should know the names of all my tenants.'

He needed to get out of the house, away from the young woman who was slowly but surely taking over the role of mistress of Blakely Hall. He had married her to provide security and love for his children, but his brains must have been addled when he proposed. His injury had left him not in his right mind.

He should never have allowed another to take over his beloved Anna's position here.

* * *

Eleanor felt the all-too-familiar tears behind her eyelids. She had become a veritable watering pot since arriving at Blakely Hall.

144

Affection was developing between herself and her husband. Foster, although loyal to a fault, had let slip on more than one occasion that Bentley's first wife had been his true love. Alex had vowed when she died in his arms he would never love another and would always remain true to her memory.

The pen snapped in her hands and she looked down in disgust at the blots spoiling her neat list. Botheration! She would have to begin again on the note of repairs and refurbishments that, in her opinion, were necessary to make this vast establishment a home. The mice had got into much of the bedroom furniture and mattresses and bed hangings must be renewed. Everywhere needed a thorough cleaning.

The clock struck the hour. The children were returning from their walk with their nursemaid. They burst into the small drawing-room Eleanor had taken as her own domain.

'Here you are at last, my loves. Come and sit down, we have much to talk about.'

Lucy dropped onto a footstool whilst Elizabeth and Alexander climbed up onto the window seat.

'Mama, can we have a water race?' Alexander shouted. Elizabeth pushed her little brother and he fell with a thud to the floor. Before they could start squabbling, Eleanor stepped in.

'Enough of that. We shall not get this finished in time to send out the invitations if you two fuss over everything.' Immediately they scrambled back, each giving her an angelic smile. 'I think, Lucy, we shall have a three-legged race, a race wearing hats, a backward-walking race, a tug-of-war, plus the ball at the wicket event. That's more than enough for one afternoon. Are you satisfied with this selection?'

Lucy jumped up and flung her arms around Eleanor. 'I would not care if we had no games at all. I've never had a birthday party, at least not one that I can remember. Cook said she's making me a cake that will have candles on, one for each of my years.'

'I know, my love, and you shall have gifts from us. However I think it's appropriate for you to give something to the village children and not the other way around.'

The child's face fell. 'What shall I give them? I do not believe I have enough toys in the nursery for everyone.'

'No, my dear, you misunderstand me. Your papa and I shall organize the gifts for them.'

By the time the children had gone upstairs for tea, Eleanor had all the information she required. Their father, in her opinion, was not taking sufficient interest, but perhaps on the day he would feel differently. They were to dine together tonight, and her new golden silk dinner gown was waiting on the rail.

Sally greeted her with a cheery smile. 'I was about to send out a search party, my lady. It's only twenty minutes before you're due downstairs.'

'That is ample time. I'm looking forward to wearing this ensemble. I was so pleased the first of my garments arrived this morning. I shall be able to dress appropriately for the first time tonight. I've never had so many beautiful gowns in my entire life and it seems a shame not to start wearing them.'

She wasn't sure how she would manage the demi-train; Sally had shown her how the ribbon slipped over her wrist to keep the material from under her feet.

'I am not sure even with the extra boning, Sally, that this dress is entirely right. Such a low neckline is meant for someone with more curves than I have.'

'You look a picture, my lady. I doubt anyone at Tendring Manor would recognize you now.'

This encouragement was enough to give her the confidence to glide down the stairs. She nodded to the footman on guard in the vast entrance hall. On walking into the drawing-room, she was surprised to find her husband absent. The previous occasions when they had dined together, he had been waiting for her. Was he brooding about the party next week? She walked to the window which faced the lake.

Good gracious! What was he doing out there staring across the water?

Without a moment's hesitation she ran along the corridor and out through the door at the far side of the house. She was wearing evening slippers, and this was a new gown which could be ruined by her foolishness. Such things meant little to her. She was breathless by the time she was in hailing distance of the figure beside the lake.

He heard her approaching. He turned when she was still a few yards away. For a moment he stared at her as if seeing her for the first time. His eyes were dark. The lines on either side of his mouth seemed more deeply etched than usual. To her amazement, his expression changed. His eyes were lit by something she didn't understand; his smile stopped her dead in her tracks.

'My dear, whatever are you doing out here? I should have joined you presently.'

His voice was strangely husky. She wanted to say something, to move toward him, but her feet remained firmly planted in the grass.

He closed the gap, holding out his hands. She didn't want to take them, but her hands moved of their own volition. The warmth of his fingers sent shock waves up her arms. Why was he looking at her so strangely? Why were his eyes glittering with an odd light? Inexorably, she was drawn closer to him. His heat pulsed towards her, his distinctive lemon scent filling her nostrils.

What was he doing?

'Eleanor, look at me. I want to see your face.'

She couldn't help herself. Her head tilted and she was staring into his eyes. Holding her with one arm around her waist, he cupped her face with his other hand. His fingers traced the outline of her lips and she trembled.

Things were changing between them. She was rapidly losing control of the situation. Her hand rested on his chest which was burning. She wanted to protest, to demand to be set free, but instead her other hand moved to his shoulder. His evening jacket was rough beneath her fingers. She slid her hand up, wanting to touch his skin as he was touching hers.

The arm around her waist tightened. She was lifted. Her feet dangled. Then without warning, his mouth pressed against hers. Her world rocked. Nothing in her life had prepared her for the exquisite sensation of a man's lips upon her own. Her head spun and heat pooled in the core of her being. Her hands entangled in the hair at the base of his neck.

His mouth brushed gently across hers, the kiss light. She wanted more, something other than this gentleness. Her lips parted and she returned the pressure. His arms tightened, crushing her against his chest. His hand caught the back of her head, holding her still. His lips became more demanding, the tip of his tongue outlining the contours of her mouth. This intimacy was too much. Panic swamped her passion and she began to struggle. Her hands pummelled his chest and she closed her mouth, forcing her head backwards.

'Put me down at once! This was not part of our bargain. I have no wish to be treated in this way.'

His colour was hectic, his eyes, no longer blue, but almost black. His hold relaxed and she was set down. Immediately she spun away, her breath rasping in her throat, her distress painfully apparent. Instead of leaving her to recover, a warm hand rested lightly on her shoulder. She flinched, but it was not removed.

'Come, my dear, you must not distress yourself. You're my wife. Whatever we agreed at the outset, surely sharing a moment of intimacy together is a good thing?'

She stepped away from him. 'Are you saying, sir, that you wish to make this a true marriage? That I am to be . . . ' Her cheeks burned a second time.

'If you do not wish me to make love to you, my dear, you should not appear dressed as you are. I had no idea you were such a desirable woman. What a difference a new gown can make.'

How dare he talk to her as if *she* was of no account? As if clothing was all that mattered, not who was *inside* the fine garments. Her embarrassment was replaced by righteous indignation.

'I have no wish to share my bed with you, my lord. Neither have I any wish to repeat this experience. I came out because I was concerned that you might be unwell. I was sadly mistaken — '

His shout of laughter sent the moorhens diving for cover. 'God's teeth! You thought I was about to throw myself into the water?'

Eleanor was about to deny this, but it had indeed been what she had feared. He had looked so desolate when he had left her earlier in the day. 'Of course I did not. I no longer wish to discuss this. I have ruined my new gown for nothing.'

His eyes crinkled at the corners; she was being laughed at. 'I'm sure you will have others arriving very soon, my dear. Your gown is far from ruined, a little grass around the hem will soon brush off. Having given any staff in this vicinity an entertaining spectacle, might I suggest we go in for our dinner? The meal will be beyond saving if we linger out here much longer.'

He took her hand and pushed it through his crooked arm, making sure she was unable to remove it. Reminded that they were in full view of anyone who cared to look from the windows, she decided to go in without protest.

'The weather has been surprisingly warm today, let us hope it continues this way until the party.'

'I have no wish to discuss the weather. In fact I have no wish to talk to you at all.' She sounded churlish and his chuckle only added to her annoyance. Sydney waited to greet them when they reappeared in the hall.

'Dinner is served, my lord, my lady.'

Alex bent and whispered in her ear. 'Now we are in his bad books, my dear. No one ever keeps dinner waiting.'

Eleanor couldn't help herself; she pressed

her free hand across her mouth trying to hold back her giggles. They were escorted frostily to the dining-room where two footmen jumped forward. As usual, they were seated at either end of the vast table which made conversation all but impossible.

'This will not do, Sydney. I am heartily sick of being obliged to shout if I wish to speak to Lady Bentley. Lay a place at the other end. Do it now.'

He stalked around the room and waited imperiously whilst a nervous footman pulled out his chair. He looked so autocratic, so fierce, but then he caught her eye and winked before resuming his glare. She had to snatch a napkin in order to bury her face and hoped Sydney believed she was suffering from a fit of coughing. Alex was difficult to resist when he was being playful and charming.

Before the meal drew to its close, she knew she was in danger of becoming emotionally entangled with her husband. Foster had told her he had a *chère amie* in London. High time he returned to his mistress. She had no wish to be used as a substitute. Unless Alex was in love with her, she would remain celibate. As this would never happen she was resigned to life as his companion only.

★　★　★

153

Two weeks after Eleanor's defection, Jane was still locking the communicating door between their rooms. Edward could hardly kick it open in someone else's house. Things would be different when they returned to the marital home. There her screams of protest would go unremarked. The servants had been hand-picked by him. All were loyal to him and would do his bidding regardless of how unpleasant the duties might be.

He was to travel back to London with a crony of Haverstock's. He had arranged this lift by being at his most charming and the poor fellow had been obliged to agree.

Thankfully there were no mewling brats to spoil the journey. Sir Anthony Deaver and his wife were in their middle years, their progeny departed for lives of their own.

He smiled across at Lady Deaver and she simpered. 'I must thank you again, my lady, for allowing me to intrude on this journey. I have urgent business in town and did not wish to discommode my dear wife and our children by dragging them there.'

'How kind of you, Lord Thorrington. Your wife must much appreciate your consideration in these matters.'

'Indeed she does; we are the most devoted couple. I cannot wait to return in order to spend time at home with her. My boys are leaving for school very soon. I wish to be there to escort them.'

She simpered again. 'How thoughtful. How thoughtful it is of him, is it not, Sir Anthony?' Her husband grunted; he was already more asleep than not. The journey was going to be tedious in the extreme, but the carriage was comfortable and no doubt the overnight accommodation would be excellent. Edward's man, Hudson, was on the box, keeping an eye on the trunks.

He settled back, closing his eyes in pretence of sleep. This would stop the wretched woman from talking to him. His head was churning. He had received an urgent summons from his lawyers. He ground his teeth. Why must he go to them each time? He had no choice for without their co-operation he would not have access to Eleanor's inheritance.

The next quarter's rents were due in less than a month, thank God. He would then be solvent and have no need to go cap in hand to the black crows who controlled the trust fund.

Odd how the children had managed to remain all but invisible these past few weeks. Something was not right; whenever he appeared in their vicinity they melted away. Unless he had been prepared to tramp up to the attics to see them, which he was not, he had been denied their company.

In the weeks since Eleanor had run away there had been a change in the way things were. It was as if the ground beneath his feet was beginning to crumble, his unassailable position of authority somehow pushed off balance by this unexpected defiance.

He had decided to let Eleanor settle in to her employment for a few weeks. If he had left before the end of the appointed time at Bridgeton Abbey there would have been comment. This was the last thing he wished. There was no danger for a few months. She would not be five and twenty until February next year; then she got control of her money. She was a plain woman, as thin as a rail, her eyes dull and her hair worse. How could someone like this attract a man of Bentley's inclination?

He had made judicious enquiries amongst the guests and learnt, to his satisfaction, that Bentley kept a mistress in town. She was the relic of a very wealthy banker, and although unsuitable to marry into the nobility was ideal in the role she had chosen to play.

From what he had heard, Bentley had vowed never to remarry. He was still mourning his first wife. If the man satisfied his carnal desires with his mistress, what possible reason could he have to marry again?

He had the required heir, so the need to procreate did not arise.

No, he was worrying unnecessarily. When he had concluded the business with the lawyers he would travel incognito to Suffolk and find out how things stood for himself. Eleanor could stay where she was for a few weeks, but, my God, she would be back under his control long before February.

His man of affairs, Johnson, who was privy to everything he did, was already on his way to Blakely. This was a small village not far from the market town of Ipswich. There he was to meet with his man. When the time came, together they would plan his strategy and set in motion what was needed to remove his sister.

The following morning he marched into Messrs Thomas & Puxton in Bond Street and was shown immediately to the senior lawyer's room. This charlatan was the son of the lawyer who had dealt with his family's affairs for years. The man was about his own age, and although punctilious and polite, did not treat him with the deference he deserved.

A stooped clerk rushed to fetch him a chair. Puxton bowed. 'Pray be seated, my lord. I am glad you were able to visit so promptly.'

The man was definitely gloating. 'Get on

with it, man. I haven't got all day to sit here.'

'I have heard from Lord Bentley's lawyers. I'm sure you know the reason for this communication.'

Why in the devil's name did Bentley's legal team wish to contact . . . ? There could be only be one reason. It couldn't be true. A weight settled on his chest. He had difficulty asking the question. 'He has *married* Lady Eleanor?'

'Did you not know this, my lord? I'm sorry if this information is a surprise to you.' The lawyer glanced down at the paper in front of him. 'They were married on August seventh at Bridgeton Abbey, the domicile of Lord and Lady Haverstock, in Hertfordshire.'

There was a rushing noise in his ears. His head spun. The bitch had married Lord Bentley before she left. He had been told a fabrication. Everyone had been laughing at him behind his back. Bile rose in his throat and an overwhelming rage consumed him.

'If you would sign here, Lord Thorrington; and please place your initials at the bottom of these other pages.'

Edward scrawled his name with a flourish; it would not do to let the lawyer know exactly how he felt about this matter. Bentley had insisted he sign over Eleanor's trust fund and he had no choice but to concur. In return his four children had received a sum of ten thousand pounds each to be held in trust by the lawyers until they were of age. The interest was to be added to the account; the money was unavailable to him.

'Was there anything else?'

'No, my lord.' The man folded the duplicate document, fussily tied pink ribbon around it, and handed it to him. 'This is an excellent match. I'm sure you must be delighted to see her so well settled, my lord.'

Edward ground his teeth. 'I am indeed, sir. She will be sorely missed at Thorrington Manor. She was a second mother to my children.' He stood, bringing an end to the tedious conversation.

He would spend a pleasant evening in the company of his mistress. Helen was always enraptured by his presence. He had arranged for his carriage to collect him from his town house the next day. It was high time he returned to the bosom of his family. His wife had still not been taught that defying him always led to pain and misery. Eleanor had learned that lesson well.

London was hot and there was an outbreak of infectious fever in the East End. Would his health be at risk when he travelled through that district in order to return to Essex? His lips curved in a facsimile of a smile.

There was a possible way he could benefit from this catastrophe. Eleanor was the wife of a wealthy man; if her husband died it was possible the Bentley brats would be placed under his guardianship.

When that man died she would receive her inheritance intact. He had been surprised to find Bentley had insisted this codicil be added to the settlement, but it suited him very well.

He would set matters in motion immediately. His man, Hudson, could handle the arrangements for him.

In a better humour, he arrived at the small house near the river where Helen resided. Whilst there he could forget his worries; his mistress didn't question his judgement or go out of her way to anger him. It was getting dark when he finally left her bed, determined to complete the task his wife had set him.

'My lord, must you leave so soon?' She stretched out a soft, plump arm and smiled enticingly. He was spent. Making love to her three times in as many hours was an exhausting business.

'I'm not coming back to bed; I'm supposed to be seeking out a governess for the children.' But Helen was very persuasive and he didn't leave her apartment until the following morning.

★ ★ ★

On arriving at Tendring Manor his wife greeted him softly. 'My lord, I'm pleased to see you home. Are you well? I . . . '

'Well enough.' He pushed past her and strode into the drawing-room. As soon as she was through the door he slammed it.

'My lord, I do most humbly beg your forgiveness for my defiance. I can't think what possessed me.'

'I will not be disobeyed. Is that quite clear?'

She cowered against the door. He raised his hand and struck her across the face.

She slid to the floor, blood trickling from her split lip. He bent down. 'I said, is that quite clear?'

She nodded and tears mixed with the blood on her cheeks. A pathetic sight. 'Enough, Jane. I forgive you. Get up, I have good news for you.'

He turned his back whilst she struggled to regain her feet. 'I spoke to a friend of mine at my club and he has recommended someone for the position of governess. Her name is Smithson. I have seen the woman's references and appointed her. I hope that is in order?'

'Thank you, my lord. I'm sure she will be exactly what we want for the children. When it she to arrive?'

'Two days from now. Make sure the accommodation is prepared and the children ready to receive her.'

12

Alex was making a particular effort to be charming and pleasant. He appeared in the schoolroom to join in the morning's lessons, played cricket in the afternoon, and promised that he would begin teaching Alexander and the girls to ride as soon as he had purchased suitable mounts for them.

There was no further intimacy, but on several occasions, especially when Eleanor was dining with him, she caught a decided gleam in his eye as he watched her across the table. She had not repeated the error of wearing an evening gown. She appeared each time in a high-necked dimity, better suited to the afternoon. Her only concession each night was a more elaborate arrangement of her hair.

The house was fully staffed; with his permission she had asked the housekeeper, Hudson, to start a thorough cleaning of the empty rooms. The day before the party, he asked her to join him for a stroll whilst the children were out with the nursery maids.

'There is something I particularly wish to show you, my dear. Also, there are matters that we need to discuss pertaining to the event tomorrow.'

'Everything is organized, I have biscuits for the village children when they go and the cake is iced.'

He grinned. 'I have no wish to know the details, my dear, merely what my duties are to be.'

'You are to wave the flag at the commencement of each race. Foster is to be the judge; I thought he might seem more impartial to the participants. At the end you are to present the winners with a silk rosette and a silver threepenny bit. Then the second a green rosette and one penny, finally for the third child a blue rosette and a halfpenny. There, that is not too arduous, is it?'

'Excellent. Come, we shall converse of something more interesting.'

'Well, my lord, I have removed the hangings from the — '

'Please, no more domestic detail, Eleanor, I beg you. These matters are your responsibility. I have no wish to be involved. Did I not see several boxes arrive yesterday? Surely you would rather talk about new clothes than bed hangings?'

She smiled. There was that strange light in his eyes again. 'I had thought that my apparel would be of even less interest to you, sir. I have more outfits than I shall ever have occasion to wear. As we do not entertain, and I am not intending to pay morning calls, why do I need so many?'

'You are a wonder, my dear. I cannot believe there's another woman in the land who would object to having a full closet. I like to see you dressed as befits your station. You are an earl's daughter, the title is your own. It was disgraceful Thorrington obliged you to wear the garb of a servant.'

This was the opportunity she had been waiting for. 'Alex, I wish to discuss my former life. The only thing marring my happiness is the fact that I've had no word from my nephews and niece. I was like a mother to them and there is not a moment in the day I do not worry about their welfare.'

He raised his eyebrows. 'Then you must invite them to visit, my dear.' He paused, his eyes watchful. 'I'm leaving for Town the day after tomorrow. I shall be away a week; I should be pleased if you had company in my absence. Why not write today and invite your sister-in-law and her children to come?'

She pressed his arm. 'Thank you, Alex. I shall write immediately.' He placed his own over hers and her heart skipped a beat.

'It's my pleasure, my dear.' He had remained with them far longer than expected;

she had no complaints on that score. The children had learned to love their father; he was no longer a stranger to any of them.

'Indeed, if they came straight away the boys could travel from here to their school.' Eleanor moved forward, forcing him to release her.

The stable clock struck three; the children would be back soon with the comfits and bonbons ordered from the village shop. Why was he leading her in this direction?

His arm encircled her waist and he guided her under the archway leading to the yard. 'Go to the third loose box, from the end, my dear.'

As he spoke a dapple grey head appeared over the door. 'What a pretty horse; I have not seen her before.' She stroked the animal's ears, loving the silky feeling.

He was beside her, patting the animal's gleaming neck. 'This is Silver, she's my wedding gift to you.'

Her hands froze. Time stood still. A gift? This was quite unexpected. 'I am obliged, Alex. I have not ridden since my mother died. However, it would be a pleasure to do so again, especially on this lovely mare.'

His shoulder was solid against hers; even through the thickness of his jacket and shirt she could feel his strength. 'I'm glad that you like her, my dear. She's perfect for you: good-natured, but eager to go.'

He was waiting for her to say more. 'Thank you, I don't expect to be given gifts. This was not part of our arrangement.'

His breath brushed her cheek, the deep brim of her bonnet couldn't protect her from this intimacy. 'Not part of our arrangement? I believe that's also something that needs further discussion at some point.'

With this cryptic comment, he took her elbow and guided her round to the home paddock situated behind the stables. In it were three brown ponies, identical in size and colour.

She couldn't restrain herself, she squeezed his hands a second time. 'The children will love them, they are perfect. Exmore ponies make the best mounts for beginners. I can't wait to get them started; they will be so excited.'

She attempted to remove her hands, but his fingers tightened. 'I thought to give them all a name day gift; I have been remiss in my duties in that respect. As they are sharing the party, I believe Lucy will be happy for her siblings to receive something as well.'

Why was he staring at her again in that disturbing way? Eleanor tried again to extricate her hands. He was so close his body heat washed over her; his familiar aroma of lemons was now mixed with saddle soap and leather.

Running feet approached the paddock. She jumped away. Davies, the estate manager, skidded to a halt. 'My lord, you must come, there's trouble in the village.'

'I'll come at once. Please excuse me, Eleanor, my dear.' Alex strode off, leaving her alone with the ponies. Presumably it was no concern of hers. She would remain a while longer before she returned to the house.

Good grief! The village! The children were there. Could this difficulty involve them in some way?

She spun, gathering her skirt in both hands, and ran after her husband, determined to discover for herself if their children were in danger. There was pandemonium in the stable yard as grooms frantically saddled horses. Alex was talking urgently to a young man, who raced off in the direction of the house.

'Lord Bentley, tell me, has something happened to the children? Has there been an accident?'

Grim-faced, he turned to her. 'You must not concern yourself, my lady. Go back to the house, I shall return later with the children. Please don't worry.'

He vaulted onto his huge stallion, the three grooms followed, plus Davies. One groom led an extra horse. This must be for Foster; the message had been sent to him.

Eleanor was not prepared to let them go without her. Lucy, Elizabeth and Alexander were her children too; she loved them as much she loved her niece and nephews. Whatever his instructions, she would not be left behind. She called to one of the remaining grooms.

'Saddle Silver at once, bring her round the front of the house. I shall be ready in five minutes.'

★   ★   ★

Alex was relieved to see Foster leaping down the marble steps and racing towards him. 'Come on, man, there's not a moment to lose. Some villain has abducted my son.' Stretching out his hand, Foster tossed over a brace of pistols, one after the other. He jammed them in his pockets. 'Are they primed and ready to go?'

'They are, my lord.'

He urged his horse into a reckless gallop scattering gravel as he thundered down the drive and into the winding lane that led to Blakely village. His stomach churned. Why should anyone snatch his son? He swallowed. Was Alexander to be held for ransom? No one in his demesne would do such a thing, here his tenants were well fed. Perhaps itinerants had drifted on to his land and snatched this opportunity.

How in God's name did they know who Alexander was? He could have been any gentleman's son. Did someone in the village point him out? Had these bastards seized the opportunity and only discovered their good fortune afterwards?

The message said nothing about the children's whereabouts, the man had spoken his piece and vanished. And what of his daughters? Why was there no mention of them? He was to go to Bunton's farm, at the far end of the village.

He raised his arm as they reached the outskirts of Blakely. To ride pell-mell down the winding main street was foolhardy. Subterfuge was called for. When his men were beside him he explained what he intended to do.

'I shall ride in; I want Tom with me. Foster, take two men and follow the path behind the church; keep hidden, and work your way toward the farm. Davies, you take the other man and follow the stream. With luck they'll not be expecting to be attacked from three sides. Go carefully, we're not sure how many we're dealing with.'

He waited until they were out of sight, then with Tom behind he resumed his ride up the deserted lane. Where was everyone? What was going on here? Were they dealing with more than just a couple of vagabonds hoping to make a few guineas?

'Tom, can you remember exactly what the messenger said? Did he ask for me in particular?'

'He did, my lord. 'Tell Lord Bentley we have his son. He's to come immediately to Bunton's barn if he wishes to recover him alive.' Those were his exact words.'

This was no random kidnapping. Why should anyone wish him harm? He had no enemies, but someone had targeted him by snatching his child. He was following their orders without a second thought. Who had known he was in residence, had known he wouldn't stop to consider the consequences?

Was it Alexander they wanted, or himself? Whoever was behind this was well-informed to have known the children were in the village today. He must concentrate. Try and fathom this conundrum before he reached the farm.

The sound of his horse's hooves on the cobbles announced his coming as nothing else could. The few shops were shuttered, the path as empty as the street. His tenants wouldn't hide without good reason. Whoever sent him the message must have terrified the villagers into doing their bidding.

If he was murdered who would gain from his death? The hair on his forearms stood up. He had told Eleanor last week he had altered his will in her favour. The estate was entailed, but his various investments would come to her. In the event of his death she would be a wealthy woman indeed. His fingers tightened on his reins and Lucifer stopped.

They had reached the turning into the narrow lane leading to Bunton's barn. Distracted by his appalling speculations he turned the animal's head and moved up the track. He must be mistaken, each day he spent in her company he liked her better. He would trust her with his life.

The hideous crack of a rifle shot jerked him from his reverie. The bullet whistled past his head, taking his hat with it. In one smooth movement he rolled from the saddle and into one of the ditches running on either side of the track. His pistols would be no use against a rifle, but he felt happier with them in his hands.

A fusillade of bullets thudded into the ground and he crouched lower. The smell from the dank water made him gag, but kneeling in human excrement was better than being dead. 'Tom, are you hurt?'

'I ain't, sir, but it was bloomin' close.'

'The horses?'

'Gone, my lord. I don't reckon either of them was hit. What do we do now?'

Alex knew they were pinned down. It was only a matter of time before their attackers appeared to capture them. Were they attempting to kill him? Or were these warning shots? Was the abductor showing him how well prepared they were?

Davies and Foster carried shotguns, but even they would be no protection against one well-aimed rifle. He had no choice; he must remain where he was, wait and see how matters developed.

Christ! How could he be so stupid?

They did not have Alexander. They would not have taken just one child; they could have taken all three. This was a ruse to get him here.

'Tom, we must crawl back down the ditch. Keep your head down. Good luck.'

★ ★ ★

'Sally, are you there? I need my habit; quickly help me change. I have to get to the village, I'm sure something has happened to the children.'

Thankfully her maid didn't argue, and in

less than the allotted time Eleanor was downstairs. Her mare was waiting patiently at the foot of the steps. The groom tossed her into the saddle. He had brought a second horse as he intended to accompany her.

'My lady, his lordship's gone to the village because a message came saying Master Alexander had been abducted.'

Eleanor's hands tightened and Silver threw up her head. 'We must make haste. I knew my children were in danger.' She gathered the reins, dug in her heels and the horse responded, breaking into a smooth canter.

She had visited Blakely many times and knew most of the villagers by name. There was a single street with the church and vicarage at one end, these stood at the end of their drive. The village green and duck pond were at the far end of the village.

She pulled Silver back to a walk as they passed the church. It might be better if they left the horses in the church yard and approached by the back lane. She dropped from the saddle and pulled the mare's reins over her head. She needed to be calm, not show the groom her fear.

'We must leave the horses here, they will come to no harm within the walls of the cemetery.'

'Shall I bring my cudgel, my lady?'

'Yes, do so. It's Jim, is it not?'

The young man nodded. 'Do you know where we're going, my lady?'

'I shall go and speak to Mrs Milner, the seamstress. Her cottage is in the very centre of the village, whatever happened she must have seen it.'

The village was too quiet. The usual sounds of activity, of dogs barking and children playing, were frighteningly absent. Eleanor shivered. She was glad when she arrived at the rear gate of the cottage she sought. She threaded her way through the vegetable patch, past the privy and washhouse, to the back door.

She knocked once; there was no sound of footsteps hurrying to answer her summons. After her second knock she heard movement and the door was pulled open a crack. A white face peered around.

'My lady, whatever are you doing here? It's a bad day, you should have stayed safe at home. Come in, quickly before you're seen.'

An arm shot out and she was pulled inside; Jim was a left to fend for himself. 'Mrs Milner, what's going on?'

'My lady, I can't tell you how dreadful things have been; I've never seen the like. At least a dozen or more men, armed to the teeth they were. Three on horseback, the rest on foot. They ordered us to shut up shop, to stay inside or be killed.' The woman mopped her eyes. 'They murdered my little Peggy. Right in front of me, they clubbed her to death because she barked at them.'

'How dreadful! Have they harmed anyone else, do you know?'

'There was deal of shouting and door banging, my lady. I don't know if anyone else was murdered.'

Eleanor took a deep breath and sent a fervent prayer to the Almighty that her family was safe. Mrs Milner was too distraught to be questioned further. The sound of cups rattling on their saucers heralded the arrival of a tray of tea. A slightly more resilient parlour maid appeared.

'Josie, exactly what we need. Put the tray down here.' She waited until the girl had lowered her burden, worried she might drop it. 'Did you see anything out there? Do you know where these men are now?'

The girl began to pour the tea but more liquid went in the saucer than the cup. 'I reckon they looked like ex-soldiers, my lady. The man who led them was well-dressed, wearing smart coat and boots. I couldn't see his face because his hat was pulled down low.'

'Do you have any idea of the whereabouts of my children when these men arrived?'

'Master Alexander wanted to feed the ducks before they returned home. I saw them walking towards the pond. That was a good few minutes before those varmints arrived.'

'Thank you, Josie. Shall I take my tea? Give Mrs Milner plenty of sugar, she needs the sweetness to recover from the shock.'

Whilst Eleanor sipped her tea, she reviewed the information. There was something she could not quite grasp, something important. Yes, she had it. Why did the message only mention Alexander had been abducted? These villains would have taken all three children, not just her son. The children must be safe somewhere. Mentioning the boy's name had been a ruse to draw Alex into the village.

Her tea slopped onto her lap. There was only one person would wish to harm her husband. Edward must know about her marriage and believed by killing her husband he could somehow retain her inheritance. Her brother was insane. His rage and disappointment had tipped him over the edge.

She should never have married, knowing Edward was given to murderous rages. She should have warned Alex, but she had been so content these past few weeks she had pushed all such thoughts out of her mind.

Now it was too late. For a second time she had put his life in peril.

13

Alex emerged cautiously from the noisome ditch. The rifle fire was concentrated at the far end where he had tumbled from his horse. His assailants didn't know they'd moved. Maybe they thought someone as top lofty as himself wouldn't crawl through excrement to escape.

Keeping low, he ran across the lane and plunged into the hedge that bordered it. The stench he brought with him meant he couldn't rap on a door and ask for assistance. Until he smelled better, he must lurk in an outbuilding and hope his own men found him first.

He crawled through the hedge and, knowing he was no longer a target, straightened. Tom arrived moments later. He visibly recoiled when within a few yards.

'I know; I crawled through a midden. I take it you were more fortunate.'

'Blooming hell, my lord, if you pardon me saying so, I ain't never smelt nothing like it.'

'The duck pond's not far from here, I'm going to immerse myself in that. Here, lad, take my pistols and keep me covered. I can't think straight until I am less noxious.'

He was in the trees at the far side of the pond checking he wouldn't be seen from the barn when Davies hailed him from the shadow of a building a few yards away.

'My lord, we heard shooting. We were about to come to the barn when we spotted you.' The man's eyes widened and he appeared to choke. 'Good God! You smell . . . '

'I am well aware of that, Davies, I don't need reminding. I'm going to wash the worst from my person in the duck pond. Tom has his pistols at the ready. Is the shotgun loaded?'

'It certainly is, sir. Go ahead; until you're cleaner we've no hope of approaching our target safely.'

The pond water was as good as a bath. A small flotilla of ducks paddled over to investigate and eagerly gobbled up the lumps that floated away. His boots were full of water; far better that than liquid sewage. He sniffed his jacket sleeve — a great improvement, although he would never wear any of these garments again.

He approached his men with a wry smile. 'Will I do, Davies? I squelch instead of stink, but hopefully I am more bearable.'

'I thought you were captured, sir. Did they not wish to parley? How are you to get young

Master Alexander back if they won't let you near enough to negotiate?'

'I don't think they have my son hostage. They want me. I was lucky not to have been killed.' He faced the ring of incredulous faces. 'Look, the bullet grazed my temple.' He parted the hair on his forehead, revealing the graze mark.

'Bugger me! That was a close call, my lord.'

'Indeed it was, Davies. Now, listen carefully. I'm certain they don't have my children. Remember, the message didn't mention my daughters. They wouldn't have taken Alexander and left the girls behind. So we must discover where they are. Tom, find your way back to the horses that Davies abandoned. Ride to Ipswich and raise the militia. We can't handle this without extra firepower. Fred, later on you must collect our mounts; do it without getting shot if you can.'

Tom asked directions from the estate manager and then vanished into the hedgerow. Alex led his remaining men to the safety of some outbuildings in which farm implements were stored.

'Davies, do you know who lives in that house over there?' Alex pointed to a substantial redbrick dwelling that overlooked the duck pond.

'The new doctor and his wife, my lord.

They moved in last spring when the old physician retired to Bath.'

'Unless I'm mistaken, I saw Lucy waving to me from an upstairs window. I dared not remain on open ground to confirm this. If you scaled this tree, I believe you could see over these buildings to the doctor's house.'

Fred scrambled up the trunk. 'You're right, my lord, it's Miss Lucy and Miss Elizabeth.'

'What about my son, can you see him?'

'No. Yes, they must have lifted him up. He's standing on a chair, I reckon.'

Alex sighed, his suppositions were correct. His children weren't the target; he was. He dismissed the idea of storming the barn, he was undermanned and such an action could only end in disaster. He must collect his children and return them to the safety of Blakely Hall. He employed almost fifty men, they must be enough to deter even the most determined assassin.

'One of you work your way around and reconnoitre with Foster and the others. Bring them back here, but make sure you're not seen. I'll make my way to the doctor's house and collect my children. I don't know how long we have before those bastards come looking for me.'

★ ★ ★

181

'Thank you for the tea and information, Mrs Milner. As the duck pond is on the other side of the road I shall have to go back the way I came and cross where I can't be seen.'

She left to a chorus of farewells and was relieved to find Jim waiting outside. She was about to tell him what she had heard when the air was rent by a series of rifle shots. Too late to think about the children, she must reach her husband before he was murdered.

Her riding habit had a divided skirt so she flung the trailing part over her arm and ran in the direction of the shots. Jim, taken by surprise, didn't have time to stop her. The outline of the barn was just ahead, a second fusillade echoed across the village. Was she too late? Would they listen to her pleas?

She steadied her pace and drew breath to shout, when her feet were swept out from under her and a heavy weight landed on her back. Winded, she could do no more than lie prostrate.

'For God's sake, my lady, what are you thinking of?'

'Foster, how dare you knock me down? Get off at once. Don't you see? Lord Bentley is in grave danger and I am the only one who can save him.'

He removed his bulk but kept a firm grip of both her arms as he pulled her upright. For a man with grey hair he was remarkably agile and far stronger than she was. If she kicked his shins would he let go? Then Fred and another man were alongside and her chance was lost.

'You must listen to me, Mr Foster. My brother, Lord Thorrington, is behind this dreadful business. He has learnt of my marriage and believes that killing my husband will get him control of my fortune and some of my husband's as well.'

'You're distraught, madam, don't know what you're saying. You're accusing your own brother of attempted murder. Only a mad man would become involved in such a crackbrained scheme.'

'He *is* insane, at least partially so. He will not stop until he has achieved his aim, Lord Bentley will not be safe. Edward will not be here himself, he is far too clever for that, but he will have paid others to do his dirty work. It is they who are trying to kill Lord Bentley at this very moment.'

Why didn't he believe her? What could she say to convince him?

'If I returned to him, I think that would satisfy him. This will give Lord Bentley time to think of a permanent way to stop him. I promise you, I shall not be harmed, I am the golden goose, after all.'

He swore as further shots rang out and she pretended to stumble. His hands slackened and she had her opportunity. Without hesitation she ran into the lane praying that the men with the rifles were not so evil as to shoot a woman in cold blood.

★ ★ ★

With his men close behind him, Alex made his way to the rear of Dr Stansted's house. He was expected. The kitchen door was flung open and three small bodies hurled themselves into his arms. He dropped to his knees to embrace them, surprised to find his cheeks were wet.

'Papa, you are all wet and you smell horrible,' Elizabeth exclaimed.

'I'm afraid I do, sweetheart, and now all three of you are equally pungent. We shall go home at once, but first I must speak to Dr Stansted and his wife.' Laughing, he stood up with Alexander in his arms and then placed his son back on the ground. 'Stay here with your sisters until I come back.'

'You cannot go in smelling like a pigsty, Papa.'

'You are quite right, Lucy. I can hear someone coming, so I don't need to enter after all.'

The sight of Blakely Hall at the end of the drive had never seemed more welcoming. He had Alexander on his pommel, Elizabeth clinging on behind and Lucy was riding with Davies. His youngest daughter was chattering away behind him, obviously not distressed in any way by the excitement. The two nursery maids were walking home, but he intended to send the gig out to collect them.

The sound of booted feet approaching caused a moment's alarm, but then he smiled. Marching towards him was a small army of male servants armed to the teeth with cudgels, sticks and shotguns. Tom must have returned to the Hall before leaving for Ipswich.

He reined in to greet them. 'Well done, men. It does my heart good to see such loyalty in my staff. Your diligence shall not go unrewarded, I promise you.'

The leader, his coachman Frank, touched his cap and grinned. 'We're right pleased to see you and the little ones, my lord, I can tell you.' His smile slipped as he looked down the row of horses. 'You don't have Lady Bentley with you?'

What is the man talking about?

'No, of course I do not. She's safe indoors.'

'That she ain't, my lord. She went off soon after you, taking young Jim with her.'

Alex kept a commendably blank face. 'Alexander, you must get down. Frank will carry you. We have forgotten to bring Mama home with us, how could we be so silly?'

He passed his son down to willing arms and then turned to lift his daughter from behind him. 'She will be in the village looking for you, and now I shall have to go and find *her* — like a game of hide and go seek, my love. Lucy, take your sister and Alexander to the nursery and your nursemaids will take care of you until we return.'

Lucy looked unconvinced but did as she was bid. Elizabeth ran to join her, carefully avoiding any contact with him.

'Your Mama is very naughty, I shall have firm words with her when I bring her home.' His words were meant to make them smile.

Elizabeth stared at him, eyes huge. 'You will not beat her for being bad, please say you won't?'

He flung himself from the saddle and pulled all three back into his arms. What nightmares had his children been forced to endure because of his self-pity? 'I was jesting, little ones. I should never hurt your mama, and neither would I raise a hand to any of you.'

He wished he could stay longer to comfort them, but he had a bad feeling about Eleanor's absence. He pushed the children towards the men. 'Three of you take them home, the rest follow me. I wish you to escort the nursemaids home.'

His stallion was fresh and galloped with as much enthusiasm towards the village as he had done earlier. There were horses racing his way, and one of the riders was leading a riderless animal. His heart plummeted to his boots. It was the little grey mare he had given Eleanor.

★ ★ ★

'Hold your fire; it is I, Lady Eleanor.' The noise stopped and she ran from the shelter of the hedge towards the barn. Perspiration trickled between her shoulder blades. At any moment she expected to feel the impact of a bullet in her back. A voice she recognized as that of her brother's manservant shouted for her to approach. Small consolation that she had been right and her brother was behind this attempted assassination.

'Hudson, are you mad? The militia will be here soon and then you and these men will be captured and hanged.'

'This business is none of your concern,

Lady Eleanor. We don't want you. We're after Lord Bentley.'

'Then you're to be disappointed, both he and the children are well away from here. I would advise that you do the same.' Her legs felt weak, somehow she found the courage to remain upright and keep the semblance of being unafraid.

Several armed men surrounded her, their rank odour enough to make her gag. Hudson beckoned her inside the barn. The interior was cool and dim, a welcome respite from the sun. There were three horses tethered at the far end and the smell from them was preferable to that of the men who had followed them in.

'I am willing to return with you. My marriage to Lord Bentley is a sham. If I am back at Tendring Manor, things will be as before, there is no need for anyone to be hurt.'

A slightly less repellent man walked over and whispered urgently to Hudson. He nodded, and gestured to the group behind her. 'Make yourselves scarce; you don't have much time. Go north initially, with luck you'll avoid capture.'

The militia was coming; there could be no other reason for this panic.

'I can ride astride, Hudson. I shall take one

of the horses; its rider must return on foot.'

Allowing him no chance to argue, she ran to the nearest animal. Jumping on to a convenient box she scrambled into the saddle. She hadn't ridden astride in years, but if her scheme was to be successful she had to stay on board. Unless she returned to her previous miserable existence, Alex's life would be in perpetual danger.

Her heart broke to leave the children; in the two months she had been living there she had grown to love them as her own. But if she stayed they would have no father. Her departure had to be the better choice. Whatever the outcome of today, the little ones would never be mistreated again so at least she had been of some benefit.

Hudson and the man who had spoken to him snatched up the reins of the remaining horses. 'He won't be happy, my lady. But taking you back will be better than nothing.'

With a horse either side of her she left the protection of the barn. There was no sign of any of the other riflemen, only the tainted air reminded her of their presence. Presumably Hudson would lead her north as well. She prayed it would not be across country, jumping hedges was beyond her capabilities.

★ ★ ★

This time Alex did not check his pace as he entered the village. Transferring the reins to one hand, he drew a pistol from his pocket. He saw three horses emerging from Bunton's farm, Eleanor was riding one of them. His roar of rage spurred the stallion faster. He raised his arm and took aim. He squeezed the trigger and the man on the left toppled to the ground. He dropped the useless weapon and snatched up the other. A second shot rang out and the remaining rider fell across his horse's neck.

Where are the riflemen? Why have they not retaliated?

Too late to think about that, he must reach Eleanor. Her mount unexpectedly surged forward, almost unseating her and then galloped away from him.

What the hell is she doing?

She must believe he was a villain, fear had made her dig in her heels. Leaning forward, he drove Lucifer faster. Inexorably she was being overhauled. 'Eleanor, rein back, you're safe now.'

His shout was carried away in the wind. Her horse was bolting, out-of-control, if he could not reach her soon she would fall to her death.

* * *

Eleanor heard horses galloping towards them and knew she must not allow the militia to take her. A shot was fired and the man on her left vanished; terrified, she slapped her reins, crouching lower in the saddle. Then, moments later, a second bang and Hudson slumped forward. Surely they would not mistake her for one of the assassins? Her horse took hold of the bit and matters were out of her control. She prayed she could remain in the saddle until the animal tired. Their race brought them to the end of the village.

Her eyes widened. Ahead of her was the bridge that crossed the brook. The brook was too narrow to take at speed and the water too wide to jump.

14

Alex was almost parallel with Eleanor's mount, they were less than twenty yards from the stream.

How can I save her?

Standing in his stirrups, he reached across, grabbed a handful of her riding habit and yanked hard.

She fell toward him. He released his reins, trusting his stallion's good sense. Twisting precariously, he encircled her waist and managed to throw her across Lucifer's neck. His horse stumbled. For a heart stopping moment he thought they would both crash to their deaths. Then his magnificent animal recovered, shortening his stride, turning sideways to avoid the bridge and the river bank. The beast she'd been riding, released of its burden, was able to gather itself and cleared the bridge in one jump. It didn't halt, but continued its wild gallop and vanished amongst the trees.

'Steady, boy. Lucifer, steady.' He had to rely on his voice to control the animal, both arms were needed to hold her safe. His reins were flapping uselessly around the horse's neck. He feared the animal might decide to follow the other one and attempt to jump the brook. He transferred his weight to the back of a saddle, spoke again and this time his horse dropped into a trot before halting.

Eleanor hadn't spoken to him; had he injured her by his brutal treatment?

'Eleanor, my dear, are you injured?'

No response. He couldn't dismount with her half on his lap, so gently lowered her to the ground. He watched in horror as her legs buckled; she dropped in a heap of blue velvet onto the dirt. Dismounting quickly, he knelt beside her, shocked at how still she was. She must be hurt. Gently, he rolled her over. Her face was paper white, her eyes closed and her breathing so slight it was barely discernible.

She must have sustained some terrible injury before he reached her. Was that why she hadn't made any attempt stop her horse when he called?

'Eleanor, sweetheart, there's nothing to fear, it is I, Alex; you're safe now.'

★ ★ ★

From a distance, she heard someone calling but didn't want to respond. She was safe. No one could harm her when she was cocooned in blackness. She was vaguely aware someone was running a hand over her person, straightening her legs, talking to her softly . . . lovingly. Her imagination was playing tricks. The minute she regained consciousness she would be revealed as a murderer, be blamed for what had taken place, and locked away for the rest of her life. It would be better to stay where she was, where she was safe, she welcomed the darkness as it claimed her again.

★   ★   ★

'Eleanor wake up. I'm your husband, you must come back to me. Your children need you, I need you. You must wake up.'

There was no response. She had no apparent injuries, no bang on the head or broken limbs. She should be awake, her lovely eyes smiling back at him. He still feared his rough handling had caused this collapse and not the villains who had abducted her.

There was no point remaining here; the sooner she was home, the better. The doctor could take care of her. Stansted would soon restore her senses.

Galloping horses approaching reminded him his men were not far behind. They could take care of the villains he had shot and Foster could speak to the militia when they arrived. His task was to get Eleanor home. Her head was resting heavily against his shoulder and her hair was falling around her face. He brushed it back from her cheeks; loving the silky feel beneath his fingers. He rested his fingertips under her jaw, checking her pulse. The beat was barely discernible.

Please God — not again!

With one hand under her shoulders and the other behind her knees, he braced himself against his horse. Her head flopped against his shoulder, her hands didn't reach out to grip his jacket. She was so pale it filled him with dread. Slowly he stood up, using Lucifer's bulk to assist him to his feet.

He would have to wait until someone joined him. He couldn't mount without help. The stallion stretched round his huge, black head and rubbed his whiskery nose against the unconscious girl as if willing her to wake up. 'Good fellow, will she rouse for you? Remain still; I need your support.'

The horse nudged him and then dropped his head to graze peacefully. As he stood, holding his wife, he wondered what had caused this madness. Why should anyone wish to kill him? He was worth nothing dead. Had they found him a difficult target and transferred their attention to Eleanor? Had they intended to hold her for ransom?

Whatever their plan, they'd bungled the attempt.

He would see all of them dance on the end of a rope before he was done.

No one could harm those he loved.

Loved? How had that come about?

During the two months they had been together, his feelings had changed. Against all the odds he had come to love his wife. His throat closed. He gazed at the comatose woman held close to his heart. He had believed, after Anna, he could never love again, that his first wife was irreplaceable — but he was wrong.

A heavy weight lifted from his shoulders; for the first time in four years he had something to look forward to. He had been given a second chance; without being aware of it he'd fallen in love with the most unlikely woman. He gazed down tenderly. Her honesty, her kindness, wit and humour, the way she loved his children — these things had won him over. If he had not been supported by his horse he would have been in danger of dropping his precious burden. Someone spoke to him and he was jerked back to the present.

'My lord, let me take Lady Eleanor from you. Is she badly injured? Did she fall?'

Alex gathered his wits. 'I don't know, she's

deeply unconscious. However, she did not fall. I have no idea why she's like this, I think it might be shock. Her pulse is weak but regular, I'm sure she will recover soon.'

He knew he was smiling, that his eyes reflected his joy at discovering himself so unexpectedly in love with his wife. Foster was eyeing him strangely.

'I think it best to forget about those bastards for the moment, my lord. I've sent someone to fetch the doctor. Shock can do funny things, especially to the gently born like Lady Eleanor.'

Alex stepped away from his horse; he was strong enough to stop an army single-handed. He must look ridiculously happy for a man holding an unconscious wife. Love did the most amazing things to a fellow. He had to share his news and Foster was as good as anyone to tell.

'I love her. I didn't believe this would happen again. God could not be so unkind as to take away my wife again. No, I'm certain He will not. Here — take her for me, Foster, whilst I mount.'

Alex stared at the face pressed against his shoulder, reluctant to let her go. His man stepped in, holding out his arms. 'Foster, shall you be able to hand her up to me when I am in the saddle?'

'Yes, my lord. Even a man of my age can manage that. Her ladyship weighs nothing at all.'

Alex vaulted onto his horse and leant down to reclaim her. This time he settled her comfortably in the crook of his arm and Foster handed him his reins. He clicked his tongue encouraging his stallion to move off in a gentle walk. There was too much to think about, his mind was whirling with possibilities. Then Foster's words came back to him. He was right; she weighed no more than a child in spite of her height. His heart sunk like a stone to his boots.

My God! Is this why she is unconscious? Does she have a debilitating disease that is keeping her so thin, and the shock she experienced today was too much for her delicate constitution?

He ignored the two men who were examining the bodies sprawled at the side of the lane. They deserved to die, if not by his hand then by the rope. The village was no longer deserted; there were folk going about their business and the shops were unshuttered. Life was continuing as normal. He ignored the stares and surreptitious looks; his only concern was to get Eleanor home where she could be taken care of.

Where were the men who had been

marching to his rescue? Had they returned home or were they still searching the vicinity for the villains? The lane in front of him was quiet, the trees making a cool green tunnel for him to ride through. He couldn't take his eyes from Eleanor. Her colour was better; she was asleep, trustingly, like a child in his arms.

His feelings for her were a miracle. His children adored her, they had forgotten their real mother. Anna was no longer a barrier to his happiness. He would never forget her, she was his first love, but he could finally move on and put the past behind him.

His arms tightened instinctively, holding her close. His love for her had not been a *coup de foudre* as it had been with Anna, but these past two months magic had been woven between them. She was not a beauty. No, that was untrue. Lately he'd noticed a change in her; when she smiled at him in a certain way she was irresistible.

Blakely Hall was a home once more. He no longer wished to go to London and rejoin Sarah. He would write to his mistress, tell her he had taken her advice and married someone to take care of his children. He would not mention his was no longer a marriage of convenience, this would be too cruel. He would merely explain the time had come for him to be personally responsible for his estates and not leave matters in the hands of his manager as he had done these past few years.

★   ★   ★

From the depths of her unnatural slumber, Eleanor could hear voices but she recognized none of them. It would be safer to remain still, keep her eyes closed. If she was a prisoner they couldn't question her whilst comatose.

No, she was in a bed, a comfortable bed and the smell of lavender linen surrounded her. Her head was supported by soft feather pillows, she could not possibly be in jail.

There was a movement beside her and she tried to raise her eyelids but they remained shut. Her limbs refused to move. She was imprisoned in someone else's body. An arm slipped around her shoulders and raised her, and the hard edge of a cup was pushed against her lips.

'Please, my lady, you must drink. You've taken almost nothing these past few days. You'll not get better if you don't eat or drink.'

Eleanor tried to open her mouth but the instructions from her brain failed to register and her teeth remained clenched. The anxious voices faded. The door closed and she was alone in the comforting darkness.

Good, they had gone, she could sleep. Only then was she safe. Then two hands gripped her shoulders. Someone was shaking her, demanding she opened her eyes.

'Eleanor sweetheart, this will not do. I'll not let you slip away from me. You must fight, we need you here with us, please don't give up. I love you, I couldn't survive a second loss. Wake up, darling, please.'

This voice she recognized; her husband. He needed her, was using endearments, professing to love her. Her eyes flickered open to find his face inches from her own. His eyes blazed with triumph.

'Thank God, thank God. Sweetheart, you have been unconscious for three days. And you have taken nothing. Rest against my arm and I shall give you something to drink.'

Obediently she relaxed, not questioning his actions, hardly believing someone loved her enough to take care of her. The cup was presented. The sharp sweetness of lemonade flooded her mouth and she swallowed convulsively. She hadn't realized how parched she was. She drained the cup but the effort proved too much.

'There, my love, you shall be better soon. I'll be back to see you later, rest again until I come.'

She was so tired. Her eyes drooped. Then unexpectedly he clasped her face and his lips brushed hers in the gentlest of kisses. He loved her. A warm glow flooded through her. She rested until he returned and repeated the process. This time he offered delicious vegetable broth; chewing was difficult, but she could swallow liquids well enough. Each time he murmured loving words, and kissed her briefly before departing.

★ ★ ★

She woke the following morning as happy as a lark. She was still weak, but the blood was fizzing round her body. She had never imagined she would be held tenderly in her husband's arms or that he would say he loved her. How had this happened? It was remarkable. From the moment he'd spoken to her two months ago when she and her niece and nephews were playing cricket, she had been drawn to him. She could not have married him otherwise, however desperate her situation.

Her lips curved and she stretched. Only now could she admit she returned his love. From today their marriage would be a loving union, the ghost of his first wife finally laid to rest. Not only did she have Alex, but she had three wonderful children to complete her happiness. A flood of heat engulfed her.

Good heavens!

Next year there might be an extra member of their family, a baby of her own to hold in her arms. How was it possible someone as handsome, charming, kind and loving as him had fallen in love with her?

She moved restlessly. How much longer would it be before the children came to visit? It had been an age since they'd been with her. Alex told her last night he was taking them to the stables this morning to continue their riding lessons.

Poor Lucy, her party must have been cancelled and all that planning and preparation gone to waste because of her. She must get up today and set another date for the event. She tingled from head to toe. She would be back on her feet in a day or two, and she had more to look forward to than just a children's party.

As soon as she was well enough Alex would come to her, and she would tell him she loved him and discover the secrets of the marriage bed.

There was a soft knock on the parlour door; Sally moved across to open it. She turned with a puzzled frown. 'Mr Foster wishes to speak to you, my lady.'

A band of pain tightened across her chest. The things she'd been pushing away came flooding back. Foster knew what had taken place, knew her brother had come to kill her husband. She and Alex had not talked about that afternoon; he didn't know why he'd been targeted.

When he discovered her secret he would never forgive her. Their marriage would be over before it had truly began.

15

Eleanor straightened in the armchair; she must be strong. Foster was good to have remained silent until this point. She could not ask him to lie to his master any longer. 'Ask Mr Foster to come in, please.'

He entered and bowed formally. 'I'm glad to see you well, my lady. I apologize for intruding, but I must speak to you in private.'

She gestured and her abigail retreated to the bedchamber. 'You are welcome, Mr Foster. Until you were announced I had all but forgotten what happened. No, if I am honest, I deliberately ignored the terrible incident which caused me to become unwell.' He stood, shifting uncomfortably. 'Please be seated, sir, you must tell me what has transpired these past few days.'

He cleared his throat. 'Well, my lady, no one else knows and his lordship is still of the opinion that these were opportunists; ex-soldiers passing through. He believes it's possible they heard he was in residence, and decided to try and abduct him and hold him for ransom. When that failed, they took you instead.'

'He has not thought it through properly.

His happiness these past few days has prevented him thinking clearly and has made him ignore what is perfectly obvious.' She could not go on, needed a moment to recover her composure. 'I must thank you, Mr Foster, for not revealing the truth. But there is something else you do not know.'

Should I tell him my secret?

'Yes, my lady?'

She took a deep breath and told him the true circumstances of her marriage. She waited for his condemnation.

'I'm relieved to hear your story, my lady. I've always been bothered by his lordship's behaviour. Such unpleasant conduct was out of character. It makes no never mind now.'

He didn't understand.

'I can't continue to live this lie. I must tell him everything.'

Foster shook his head. 'I shouldn't do that, my lady. Let sleeping dogs lie, if I were you. Your brother's an evil man if he thinks to gain back your inheritance in this way. His aborted attempt will not be repeated. Lord Bentley has alerted the authorities; they are scouring the surrounding area for the remainder of the gang. Unfortunately the two that were shot died before they could be questioned.'

She thought it was fortuitous they had died, for they could have revealed the truth.

She shuddered. How could she be glad that two men had perished? This nightmare was turning her into someone she didn't like. 'Will my husband be charged for killing them?'

'No, he was protecting his property.' Foster blushed painfully. 'I beg your pardon, my lady, I meant no offence. I've come to tell you that I will not disclose what I know. I have been in Lord Bentley's employ these past fifteen years; when his first wife died I thought he would go mad with grief. I can't believe the change in him this past week. I shall do nothing to endanger his happiness; you would be wise to do the same.'

Eleanor closed her eyes. Her husband believed he had assaulted her. Could she continue to deceive him on this point if she admitted her brother was behind the attack? No, it was either reveal everything or remain silent.

She had been enjoying a fool's paradise. Now harsh reality had come back to claim her. 'I have no wish to cause him unnecessary grief. You're right, Foster, I can never tell him. I could not bear to lose him now, I will make him happy in spite of this.'

Foster grinned, his craggy face looking years younger. 'A wise decision, my lady, if you pardon me for saying so. The reason for your marriage is unimportant. Nobody knows what happened, apart from you and I and those that were involved. And on the other matter, I hardly think Lord Thorrington is going to admit to what he did. I think it best it stay that way.'

'I have no choice but to agree. However, when Lord Bentley has time to consider the matter, he must realize that those men were trying to *kill* him, not take him captive. How shall you explain that to him?'

'I have thought of that, my lady. I shall tell him that they must have decided he was too fearsome a target to abduct, that he was more likely to kill them than come quietly. They aimed to scare him away, not kill him. Your arrival on the scene gave them another chance so they snatched you instead. You must tell him they threatened to kill you if you did not go quietly.'

So be it. She would be obliged to live a life based on perfidy. 'You couldn't possibly know these facts. I must tell him this fustian. I must compound my faults with falsehoods. If Lord Bentley should ever discover the truth, our marriage will be at an end. Surely it's far better to bring matters into the open now, before things have moved on?' She stopped, embarrassed at talking so freely to a servant.

'My lady, I implore you, don't consider

revealing the true facts. This would ruin his life. You can't want to bring him down again?'

'No, of course not. I just wish it could be done some other way. The children are happy now they have their father with them; I've no desire to be the one to break their hearts a second time. I shall rehearse my part and explain it to him later.'

'Thank you, my lady. In a year or two it will be as if this never happened. You will have built a happy life together and even if, somehow, he discovered the deception, it would no longer be of any importance.'

'I pray you're correct, Foster. I think you'd better go now, I don't wish Lord Bentley to know that you have been to see me.'

He rose and bowed again. 'You can trust me, my lady. Although I am his lordship's man, I would lay down my life for you as well.'

He left the room, taking her happiness with him. A weight was pressing her down, preventing her lungs from filling. She must fight this blackness or she would sink into oblivion. The sound of childish voices approaching roused her before she gave in.

The children were finally coming to visit. Whatever her reservations about lying to her husband, where *they* were concerned there were no barriers. They spent half an hour talking about their riding lessons; the new ponies were a great success. They were obviously delighted to see her well, and made no mention of the missed birthday party.

'Mama is tiring, children. Time you returned to the nursery. You may come down again and visit after tea.'

Lucy and Elizabeth obeyed their father immediately, embracing her fondly before moving to the door. Alexander, who was cradled on her lap, ignored the instruction and smiled trustingly into her face.

'Did Papa tell you he fell right into a smelly midden? He was so stinky he had to have a bath in the duck pond.'

Eleanor's eyes widened in astonishment. Her husband grinned, looking almost boyish. 'That's quite true, my dear, I'm surprised you don't remember it. I've disposed of the garments I was wearing and my favourite top boots will not be the same again.'

The little ones giggled. She returned his smile. 'I'm sure the experience was educational, sir, for there's nothing so humbling as being up to your knees in muck.'

Alex interrupted. 'Lucy, Elizabeth, Alexander, run along to the nursery; I wish to speak to your mama.'

Alexander gazed at his father, his lower lip trembling. 'I want to stay here with Mama.

She has been poorly and she needs me to keep her safe.

'No, darling, you shall see me later. Do as you're told, my love. I shall look forward to seeing you again this evening.'

The little boy was reassured. 'I shall go then, Mama, but you must promise not to be ill again. I don't like it when you're not with us every day.'

'I will do my best, darling. Off you go, your sisters are waiting for you at the door.'

The room seemed empty without them. She wasn't sure she wished to be alone with Alex. She wanted to postpone the deceit for as long as possible. However, he remained with her, strolling across to join her on the daybed. Her pulse raced, she felt something she didn't understand flickering between them.

He took her hand in his, carrying it to his mouth. His eyes held hers, he kissed each finger in turn. A delicious warmth pooled deep inside. She couldn't look away.

He raised his head, his eyes glittering, keeping her left hand in his. 'My love, we have much to talk about. First there's something I must give you.' He reached into his waistcoat pocket and removed a small velvet box with gold filigree on the front. He flicked it open revealing a stunning diamond and emerald betrothal ring. 'I love you, Eleanor, I want you to have the family ring.'

Her fingers were trembling as he pushed it over her knuckle. 'There, now you are a Bentley bride. As soon as you're well enough I wish to make you my true wife.' The love in his eyes was almost her undoing. How could she bear to keep her secret from him? 'Will I be welcome in your bedchamber, my darling?'

She couldn't answer; her throat was clogged with tears. Instead she nodded and that was all he needed. He gathered her close and the next ten minutes took her to a place she hadn't known existed — where she was loved and could be herself.

'I must stop, or I shall not be able to.' He was breathless, a hectic flush across his cheek bones and seemed reluctant to move away from her.

'Alex, I am — '

'I understand. This is a shock to me as well.' He claimed her hands, caressing her palm with his thumbs, sending shivers up and down her spine. He was so close, his words brushed her cheek.

Then the light was blotted out. His hands cradled her face, his mouth covered hers and his kiss sent shock waves through her body. This was no gentle brush of the lips, but demanding, his mouth slanting hard across her lips. She was burning, pressing herself against him, knowing she wanted something more from him but not sure what it was she craved.

Again he sighed and moved to the far end of the *chaise longue*. 'This will not do, my love. I'm taking shameful advantage of you. But having discovered I'm in love with you I want to tutor you in the pleasures of the bedroom.'

When her pulse returned to normal she swung her legs to the floor and stood up. 'I'm as eager as you, my dear, to experience everything a wife should know. However, I believe these things are best done in the privacy of the bedroom and not in full view of the staff.'

He chuckled. 'Exactly so, you have a wise head on your shoulders. Now we must converse of something mundane, turn our minds away from these exciting things.'

'There is something I wish to talk about, Alex. What happened on Lucy's birthday? Was the party cancelled?'

'Of course it was. The children were more concerned about you than anything else. The cake was cut and we gave Lucy her gifts. Alexander has his name day shortly, shall we hold the event on his anniversary instead?'

Eleanor turned away, not wanting him to see that tears filled her eyes. Three weeks was a long time; would she still be his dearest love then?

16

The sound of gentle breathing on the pillow beside her told Eleanor she was not dreaming. Alex was sleeping there; he hadn't returned to his bedchamber this time. She rolled on to her side in order to watch him.

How she adored this man! After such an unpromising start this was now a true love match.

A cockerel crowed in the distance; dawn would come soon. Her abigail knew better than to disturb her before being summoned. Reaching out, she brushed her fingers against his naked shoulder. Instantly his eyes opened and a lazy smile curled his lips.

'Good morning, my darling. Is it time for me to go?'

'Not yet, it's scarcely light.'

He yawned, watching her, his eyes reflecting that strange glitter she now recognized as passion. 'Excellent, than I have time to return to the land of nod.'

Two could play this game. She stretched, raising her hands above her head, making certain her breasts were visible through the thin cloth of her nightgown. 'I had not

215

realized; I am also fatigued.' Deliberately turning her back she made a pretence of settling into the pillows.

How long before he reached for her? Her skin twitched in anticipation of his touch. A familiar warmth rippled through her.

Waiting was unbearable.

Why did he not make love to her? Surely he hadn't gone back to sleep? Had she imagined the darkness in his eyes, the flush across his cheek bones? Unable to wait another second, she rolled back.

He was propped up on one elbow watching her, waiting to see if this time she would take the initiative. For the past four nights he had come to her, and each time they made love she had enjoyed it more. She was certain he shared her delight; it was so much harder for him to hold back than it was for her.

'Are you fatigued, Alex, my love? I am inexperienced in these matters, I would not dream of asking you to overexert yourself. After all, you are a deal older than myself, I expect a man of your advanced years — '

In one sinuous motion he was on top of her, his desire more than evident.

'Baggage! Too old indeed? You shall be the one to call quits before I leave your bed.'

★ ★ ★

What the servants thought of the fact they did not rise until noon bothered her not one jot. She rang the bell as soon as he closed the communicating door behind him. Sally appeared immediately.

'Is my bath ready? Put out my habit, we are riding this morning.' Eleanor barely contained her giggles. By the time they reached the stables it would be afternoon.

Downstairs, she met the housekeeper about her business. 'Is everything ready for the arrival of Lady Thorrington and the children tomorrow?'

'Yes, my lady. As requested I have put the children upstairs in the nursery wing, the governess in a chamber on the floor below. Lady Thorrington has the butterfly apartment; there is a small room for her maid there.'

'Thank you. Is Lord Bentley downstairs?'

'Indeed I am. I have been waiting this age for you, my dear.' He spoke from directly behind her forcing her to stumble forwards in shock. His arms clasped her waist to steady her.

Eleanor deliberately relaxed against him, knowing this would cause him to react in a most interesting way. She wondered how he would disguise his arousal in front of the housekeeper. She attempted to move away, leaving him exposed, but he tightened his grip, using her to hide his embarrassment.

'Come along, we must not keep the horses waiting any longer.'

She found herself whisked away to a side door and unceremoniously bundled outside. In full view of any gardener that might be lurking in the shrubbery he pinned her to the wall. 'I had no idea you were insatiable, my love. I had thought your passion spent this morning.'

He pressed himself closer. He was more than ready to continue their lovemaking but she certainly was not. How could he think she would wish to indulge in such a pastime outside, for heaven's sake? 'Let me go at once, Alex. I admit defeat. Now who is keeping the horses waiting?'

His mouth found hers and she returned his kiss. She had not known physical love could be so addictive. Fortunately he reined in his passion and with a final tender embrace stepped back.

'Sweetheart, you should know by now that I find you irresistible. Every moment we are apart I can think of nothing else. I'm like a green boy once more; you have given me back something I thought lost forever. I love you, Eleanor, promise me you will never leave me?'

She thought he must be jesting, but his face was serious and her flippant answer remained unsaid. 'I shall never leave you, Alex. I love you more than my own life. As I explained to you, that is why I disobeyed your orders and followed you into the village.'

'Then I must be imagining you are holding something from me. I see such sadness in your eyes it breaks my heart. I wish you could share this dark secret with me. I am here to protect you. I give you my word, you shall never be unhappy again.'

His kindness was almost too much to bear. She could never tell him her secret because then he would hate her and send her away. Foster had been wrong. The closer they became the more this terrible deceit weighed on her soul. Whatever the outcome, in the New Year she would reveal everything to him.

One Christmas with the children around them, then she would destroy both their lives. He might forgive her eventually for her lies. Keeping it from him was not an option, truth would always out. Already she knew him so well; for every month she deceived him he would hate her more. Her only chance of salvaging her happiness lay in honesty.

But not yet. However wrong it was she had decided to give herself the remainder of the year to enjoy the bliss of being loved unconditionally. Alexander had his name day in two weeks and Elizabeth's was two weeks later. She must not ruin any of these forthcoming celebrations. After all, had she not already spoilt Lucy's party?

★ ★ ★

Edward paced his study. Several days had passed with no news from Suffolk. Surely the deed was done by now? He must find out what had transpired. Why did his men not return and tell him?

Edward's temper became more fragile and his wife flinched every time he came near her. Of his children there was no sign, but then in a house this size it was perfectly possible to avoid meeting another resident if that was the desired objective. Miss Smithson's presence meant he was obliged to keep his temper in check. No doubt a relief to his wife and staff.

When Jane received a personal letter, he was tempted to remove it from her hand, but the governess was in the hall and he didn't wish to appear brutal in front of her.

'My lord, this is from Eleanor. She is so happy, it appears hers is a love match after all. She has invited myself and the children to visit, is that not kind of her?'

'When was this letter written?'

She blinked, obviously surprised by his abrupt question. 'Yesterday, sir. Lord Bentley is obliged to go to Town on business for a few days, and he suggests the children and I go to Blakely Hall. Do I have your permission, my lord?'

Bile rose in his throat. He nodded his consent, not trusting himself to speak. His well-laid plans had gone awry and yet he had employed the best he could find. The only explanation was that Hudson had turned traitor and vanished with his money.

He sought refuge in his study, his mind in turmoil. He could do nothing more until quarter day when he received his rents, he had invested everything in this first venture. Next time he would go himself.

He stopped.

Hadn't Jane just asked if she could visit Blakely Hall? The invitation hadn't included him but they could hardly turn him away if he accompanied them.

His world righted. He had no need to employ further unreliable minions; he would see to the matter himself. Perhaps there would be an opportunity to arrange a tragic accident to remove Bentley.

★ ★ ★

It took all Alex's willpower to restrain himself from making love to Eleanor right there. He had never felt this way about any other woman, not even Anna or Sarah. The first time he shared Eleanor's bed had been a revelation.

He kept his arm firmly around Eleanor's waist as they resumed their walk to the stables. For all her protests he knew there was something she was hiding from him. He guessed it was concerning her life under her brother's control. She would tell him in her own time, perhaps the visit of her sister-in-law and niece and nephews would provide the ideal opportunity.

'Sweetheart, I can cancel my visit to Town. My lawyers could come down to me this time; I could also rearrange my appointment with the Minister. I promise I shall not be *de trop;* you shall have as much private time with your sister as you wish.' She stiffened, he was sure of it. Did she wish him away from home for some reason?

'Please, Alex, do not discommode yourself in any way. Lady Thorrington is not the one I wish to spend time with. I can't wait to see my niece and nephews for I've missed them desperately.'

She looked up at him, and for a moment he thought he detected fear in her expression.

'You will be gone little more than a week. When you return we shall have the house to ourselves again. My guests will have gone back to Colchester. Edward and Jonathan must depart for school after that. This is the last opportunity I'll have to be with them. They will not wish to visit with me once they're more independent.'

'In which case, my love, I shall leave as planned tomorrow. However, I'll not stay any longer than I have to.' His lips curved and in spite of his good intentions he lifted her from her feet in order to kiss her properly.

Buckets clattering in the yard prevented the inevitable. Sliding her to the ground, his voice was constrained as he whispered in her ear. 'We shall ride to the charcoal maker's hut, it's disused at the moment.'

She was as breathless as him, her eyes dark with passion. She nodded her understanding and, leaving her hand in his, they hurried into the stable yard where Lucifer and Silver were waiting impatiently.

★ ★ ★

Eleanor's heart almost stopped when Alex suggested he not go to town. She couldn't risk him being on the premises when the children arrived. They had seen what took place that dreadful day and might let the truth slip.

She was being nonsensical. As far as everyone was concerned they and their nursemaid had been in the maze, and couldn't have witnessed her attack on Alex. Why should anyone wish to question them about that event? Still, she would be more comfortable if the Thorringtons left Blakely Hall before he returned.

She had only agreed to invite Jane and the children because she was certain Alex would be elsewhere. He had two urgent appointments to fulfil; one pertaining to the government, another with his lawyers. He was punctilious in his duties to the Crown, he would not come back until he had completed this task.

Her composure fully restored, she smiled. The glitter in his eyes caused her to miss her step. The way the grooms avoided eye contact made it perfectly clear their misbehaviour had already been relayed to the stables by an unseen watcher. Nothing happened at Blakely without it being observed by someone or other.

Alex tossed her onto the saddle and adjusted the stirrup leather himself. His long fingers lingered unnecessarily on her ankle, stroking her stockinged calf before releasing her.

If someone had said to her three months

ago she would be as wanton as a courtesan where her husband was concerned, she would have thought them fit for Bedlam. She had no idea of the whereabouts of this empty cottage; no doubt he would lead the way.

They clattered under the arch and trotted decorously through the formal garden, turning left down one of the gravelled rides and heading into the park. Lucifer was barely jogging but Silver was obliged to trot in order to keep up. She called across to Alex.

'It would seem your stallion has taken quite a liking to my mare. He seems quite content to adjust his pace to hers.'

His wicked grin made her stomach somersault. 'As I am to yours, my love. Now, shall we gallop to the woods? You take the lead, I will give you a three-minute start.'

This was the normal practice on their outings. Silver knew what was expected of her, and as soon as the reins slackened and Eleanor transferred her weight forward, the animal's muscles bunched. Silver moved smoothly into a gallop. On more than one occasion these past few days, her hat had come loose and vanished over the horizon. On the previous occasion considerable time had been spent recovering the errant item and her hair had to be repinned before they dared to return.

Crouching over the horse's withers, she

laughed from the exhilaration. Lucifer could overtake them even if he remained stationary for ten minutes, let alone three. The black nose reached her boot, edged easily ahead until they were galloping side by side. She glanced across, Alex was restraining his mount with one gloved hand, the other, the one adjacent to her, he kept free. He was ready to snatch her to safety if ever she was in danger of slipping from the saddle.

★ ★ ★

The return journey was almost as exciting as their race to reach their destination. She glowed from head to toe from their illicit love-making on the floor of the empty hut. How much she had changed since her arrival a few weeks ago. She looked sideways; he had changed as well. Over the weeks they had been together, the frown that had been perpetually upon his forehead had vanished; his mouth had an upward tilt instead of down. He laughed easily, played freely with the children, in fact was perfect in every way.

They were in the Grand Hall, several servants busy about the place, when he asked her playfully, 'My darling, did you enjoy our ride?' He raised his eyebrows slightly. She blushed scarlet.

'I did, thank you, sir. If you will excuse me, I must change out of my habit. You look quite flushed yourself, perhaps you were over-exerted during our outing. I would not wish you to do yourself harm on my account.' His laughter followed her up the stairs. She had promised to take the children down to the lake that afternoon. There was a section roped off where even Alexander could enter without fear of drowning.

That evening they dined outside again. This was an innovation she had suggested a few days before. The table was laid on the terrace as formally as if in the grand dining-room. They sat side by side in front of the damask-covered table; crystal sparkling, silver cutlery shining and the candelabra waiting to be lit if they should care to remain outside at dusk.

'I love this view, Alex. The sunlight dancing on the lake, the trees dipping down their branches as if to drink from it. I have never seen anything so lovely.'

'The park is spectacular, sweetheart. But there are other places to equal it. Far too late this year, but next spring I shall take you on a wedding trip. I have a yacht, I use it mainly when I travel on government business, but I shall have it refitted for you this winter. We shall sail to the Mediterranean where I will show you the wonders of the Parthenon, the Acropolis and the temples and churches of Rome.'

She tried to keep her smile intact. She would not be here next spring; she would have been sent away forever because he would know her dreadful secret.

That night their lovemaking was sweeter, more tender than anything that had gone before. She was desolate at the thought of him leaving in the morning and could not bear to let him go. Eventually they fell into a deep, satisfied slumber a few hours before dawn. When she woke she was alone, but there was a note on the pillow where he had laid his head.

Her intention had been to rise early and bid him farewell in person. She snatched the paper and unfolded it. He must have written it at the walnut desk in her sitting room and then returned to place it beside her. His writing sprawled across the page.

My darling Eleanor,

I know you wanted to wave me on my journey, but you were sleeping so peacefully I could not bring myself to wake you. I am leaving earlier than planned, the sooner I get my business done the quicker I can return to you.

I love you, Eleanor. You have made me happier than you can ever know. Blakely is a home again and I never want to be anywhere else but there with you by my side.

Enjoy your guests, but miss me as I shall miss you every second we are parted.

Yours eternally,
Alex

She raised the paper to her nose, inhaling deeply. Yes, she could detect the faintest tang of lemon. It was the scent she would forever associate with the man she loved to distraction.

The light filtering through the shutters was sufficient to see the mantel clock. It was a little after seven o'clock, more than time to be up and about her duties as mistress of this huge establishment. The children were as excited as she to meet their new cousins. Lucy had never had friends her own age and was delighted there would be two boys, one just a year younger than her, to play with.

Alexander was the same age as Amanda, it would be a treat for them to intermingle. Ned, at almost twelve years of age was coming into manhood, he might well find childish games beneath him. She had arranged for him to learn how to handle a bird of prey, falconry ought to be of interest to him.

Two coaches eventually rattled to a halt the other side of the little bridge over the dry moat. She was as eager as the children to greet the occupants and hurried across to wait between the carved animals that flanked the entrance. Lucy was on one side, Alexander holding her hand and Elizabeth in front, leaning against her skirt. They were not dressed in their best, she wanted them to take their cousins into the gardens and let them run around.

The first carriage, the larger of the two, must contain Jane and children. Why there had been a necessity to bring a second, she had no idea. It was possible, of course, that the governess and servants were travelling separately. Normally her brother made the servants and the baggage travel in a cart. She had been surprised they had not arrived the previous day.

Two footmen let down the steps and opened the door. Jane descended, but instead of the four children tumbling out behind her someone else stepped down. What was *he* doing here? How dared he show his face at Blakely after he had tried to murder her husband? What mischief was he planning

230

now? Thank God Alex was away from home and out of harm's way.

Her brother glanced in her direction. His smile did not reach his eyes.

17

The children jumped out of the second
carriage, accompanied by Betty and Mary.
Their exuberance more than made up for the
lack of enthusiasm her sister-in-law displayed.
Of Miss Smithson there was no sign.

Eleanor gave what she hoped was a
welcoming smile to Jane, ignored her brother,
and ran to greet her nephews and niece.

'My word, Aunt Eleanor, this is a splendid
place. It must be twice the size of Tendring
Hall.'

'I believe Blakely is at least that, Ned.' She
refrained from embracing him; he appeared
to have grown several inches and matured
beyond his years in the three months since
she'd seen him. There was a wary look in his
eyes she recognized. He was taking the brunt
of the beatings since she'd left.

Amanda threw herself into her arms,
sending Alexander flying. 'Sweetheart, be
careful, you have knocked your cousin over.
Here, Alexander, let me help you up.' With
one arm around her niece, Eleanor offered
her hand to her son.

He grinned. 'I'm all right, I like this little

girl. Has she come to be my friend?'

'Yes she has, my love. There, brush down your breeches and bow like a gentleman.'

She smiled as Amanda curtsied awkwardly and he bowed. Introductions over and protocol forgotten, he grabbed Amanda's hand.

'Come with me, little girl. I am going to lose you in the maze.' Squealing with delight Amanda allowed herself to be dragged off, hotly pursued by Mary. When the other children had made their bows Eleanor spoke quietly to Betty.

'I shall come up to the nursery later and talk to you. Betty, I am so glad to see you here. By the by, where is the governess? I expected her to be with you.'

Betty curtsied and nodded, glancing nervously over her shoulder at Lord Thorrington. 'She said she had the toothache. She's supposed to join us when she's had it pulled.'

Daisy appeared from the nursery. 'Shall I go with the children, my lady? Or shall I oversee the unpacking.'

'Daisy, you can stay out here and get to know Betty; the unpacking can be left to the juniors, there are enough of them after all. Lucy and Elizabeth, take the boys down to the maze. Show Jonathan and Peter the

233

gardens afterwards.'

Her oldest nephew was standing diffidently to one side. 'Ned, my dear, I have arranged for the falconer to come and show you how to fly a bird of prey. However, he will not be here until tomorrow morning. Could I prevail upon you to act as guardian to the little ones until then? I wish to catch up with your mama.'

His eyes lit up. For the first time since his arrival the boy she had left reappeared. 'That would be splendid, Aunt Eleanor. Thank you so much. Of course I should be delighted to take care of the children in your absence.' He squared his shoulders and marched off behind the others, very much a young adult in authority.

All this had taken barely five minutes, but it was too long. She knew her brother would be angry at being overlooked. Her stomach roiled, familiar fear threatened to swamp her, but she pushed it back. She was no longer under her brother's control. She was mistress here, could keep him waiting if she pleased. That was her prerogative

She spun and walked briskly to greet her visitors. 'Jane, I am so glad to see you at Blakely Hall.' She glanced at her brother disdainfully. 'However, I am surprised to see *you* here, Edward. I had thought you away on business this week.' That was nonsense and they both knew it.

Jane sensed Eleanor was now her protector and moved closer. Edward nodded, his lips thin, his eyes angry.

'I had thought to see for myself how my only sibling has settled herself. As I was not privileged to attend your nuptials, Eleanor, it's only right that, as your former guardian, I should reassure myself you are being well looked after.'

'That is kind of you, my lord. As you can see, I am blooming. I shall have you shown to your apartments. There will be a light luncheon served in the breakfast parlour at noon. We dine at six o'clock; my husband prefers to keep town hours even when in the country.'

She had acquitted herself well. He could not have known how nervous she was. Linking her arm through Jane's, she squeezed it reassuringly.

'Come along, Jane, we have so much gossip to catch up on. You must tell me every little thing your children have been doing since I have been gone and I shall bore you with accounts of the wonders my own have accomplished.'

Her drollery made her sister smile, but she had a nervous air as they walked across the bridge and into the small courtyard.

'This is a magnificent house, Eleanor. I'm

so glad you have found such a lovely home.'

Her brother was staring around at the edifice. By the rigidity of his shoulders it would seem he was not best pleased that Blakely was most likely four times the size of his own mansion.

'I have put you in the guest rooms closest to me, Jane. Bentley is away all week so we can spend every moment together, if that is what you would like.'

'And my husband, where is he to go?'

'He will be at the far side of the house, in the royal suite, he cannot complain that he isn't being shown the utmost respect.'

Sydney appeared and Eleanor spoke to him. 'Lord Thorrington has unexpectedly joined us. Would you have the Royal Suite prepared for him? Lady Thorrington shall remain where she is.'

The butler snapped his fingers, sending minions scurrying in all directions to do his bidding.

'Edward, there is a billiard room; a footman will take you if that is what you would like to do. If you should care to ride, there are a dozen hunters up to your weight in the stables.' She was not going to offer him access to the gun room. 'Also there are fishing rods available, and trout in the lake if you should wish to spend your time in such a gentle pursuit.'

He scowled. 'When is Bentley coming back? I particularly wish to meet him.'

Eleanor shivered, her hands clenched. There was menace behind his words.

'If my husband had known you were to accompany my sister and the children I'm sure he would have made every effort to rearrange his appointments. However, as neither of us knew you were to honour us with your presence, brother, he is detained in Town until after your departure.'

He shrugged as if it meant little to him either way. 'No matter, I shall no doubt meet him at some function in the future. You've fallen on your feet here, Eleanor. I wonder how you achieved that?'

Could he possibly know her secret? No one, apart from the children and their nanny, were aware of what had happened at the Abbey. Had he beaten the information out of Ned? Was that another reason the boy was on edge and looking so thin and strained?

There was no time to worry about such matters, she must remove Jane to her apartment, and discover if her fears about Ned were correct. Amidst a flurry of maids, footmen and trunks she led her sister-in-law upstairs. Eleanor closed the door on the bustle in the corridor. 'Sit down with me, Jane, you're shaking like a leaf. Has it been very bad since I went?'

To her consternation, Jane burst into noisy sobs. In all the time she had known her, she had never seen her sister cry. She had heard her in the privacy of her chambers many times, but this was the first time Jane had let down her guard in her presence.

'You cannot believe how dreadful it has been without you, Eleanor. Matters have been a little better since he appointed the governess, Miss Smithson. Unfortunately she has been obliged to remain behind. I hope it was sufficient to bring Betty and Mary? The children don't need to continue with lessons this week; it can be considered a holiday.'

'I noticed Ned has lost weight. Admittedly he has grown taller, but I don't like to see him pale and worried looking. Tell me, is he being mistreated now?'

Jane nodded miserably. 'Thorrington blames him for your departure; this is irrational and unfair, but it was ever thus. I keep the children away from their father as much as possible and he has been absent in Town a few times, thank God. When he's home, however, he seems to delight in abusing my poor Ned.'

'The man's a monster! You must remain here. This is a huge establishment and you could have your own apartments. We would hardly know you were here.'

Jane sniffed and blew her nose. 'That is kind of you, dearest Eleanor. I cannot. I am bound to him by law. If I remained he would take the children away from me; I could not let him do that.' She smiled. 'I must apologize for not warning you he was coming. I had no idea myself until he got in the carriage with me. I can't think why he wanted to come, he knows you're content as he reads all your letters.'

Eleanor was tempted to tell her sister-in-law the real reason her brother had come to Blakely. There was no point in alarming her further. Jane was miserable enough as it was, without knowing her husband was a potential murderer.

She closed her eyes in shock. Was there a taint in Thorrington blood? After all she had almost killed Alex. She must push these evil thoughts aside. 'It will be a relief for you when the boys go to school next week. At least away from home they will be safe.'

'Thorrington has been even stranger lately. He has been prowling around the estate these past ten days. There's something gnawing at his very soul. His manservant has left him, and another outside man has gone as well. The valet he brought with him was only appointed last week.' Jane shuddered dramatically. 'I don't like this man at all, he's even worse than Hudson. His eyes are set too close together, and he has a shifty way of looking at one; as if he knows things that I do not.'

'Presumably he was the small man travelling on the box?'

'Thorrington refused to allow my maid in the coach with us, so I refused to have his man inside. Either the valet had to travel outside or stay home. My abigail was forced to remain at Tendring Manor. I hope I can borrow your girl whilst I'm with you?'

'There's no necessity for us to share, Jane. I have a plethora of young girls all eager to show me their skills.' She leant over to ring a little brass bell on the table. When Sydney arrived, she smiled. 'Lady Thorrington has been obliged to leave her abigail behind. Ask the housekeeper to send someone suitable to her apartment.'

The next hour passed pleasantly enough. Eleanor took Jane on a tour of the main part of the house and then up to the nursery to show her where the children were sleeping. 'I, too, must appoint a governess for the girls. Alex does not wish me to teach them.' The shock on Jane's face was comical. 'I know, it's most unconventional, but he insists that I use his given name. As I was saying, he does not like me to spend as much time in the school room as I want. I have a list of suitable candidates to invite for interviews shortly. I shall oversee the children and they will spend the afternoons with me, but the mornings shall be given over to someone else.'

Jane admired everything she saw, especially the long gallery filled with books. 'I have never seen so many volumes in one place, Eleanor. I can't imagine one person could ever read all these.'

'I am working my way along the shelves, there is gold among the dross. I am never without something interesting to peruse.' Not that she'd had much time for reading since last week.

Her brother failed to appear at luncheon, which was a relief to everyone. The children, as a special treat, were allowed to eat downstairs. They spent a noisy, happy hour and even Ned seemed more relaxed. 'Ned, if you should care to ride, please take my hack out. She's the dappled grey, sweet-natured but loves to gallop and jump. She will be exactly right for someone of your size.'

He grinned. 'I've seen her, Aunt Eleanor. She's beautiful. Can I go out after luncheon, Mama? I shall stay on the park; there is so much to explore.'

Eleanor waited for Jonathan and Peter to complain at being excluded from the treat but they were too busy planning a swim in the lake with the others to worry about their older brother's activities.

'A groom must accompany you. He can make sure you don't get lost. I should hate to have to send out search parties.'

★   ★   ★

Dinner was a chilly affair. Her brother barely said a word, Jane was subdued and Eleanor had little inclination for small talk. The meal was excellent, but she ate little of it. With considerable relief she left the table and led Jane into the drawing-room. As soon as they were out of earshot, she changed direction and guided her sister-in-law toward the staircase.

'Jane, let's go upstairs, we can have tea there. I've no wish to spend the evening with my brother.'

'What about Thorrington? What shall he do on his own?'

Eleanor had no idea and cared less. With luck he would become bored without male company and take one of the carriages and return to Tendring Manor. Failing that, as long as he remained away from her and the children for the duration of his visit she would be sanguine.

The pattern of their days was repeated. The children became brown as berries. Ned, free from the tyranny of his father, became a boy again and learnt to fly a peregrine. When he wasn't riding Silver, he was swimming in the lake with the other children.

After five days the weather broke, torrential rain replacing the summer sunshine. The children moved their games inside. In order to occupy them Eleanor set up a treasure trail for the children to follow. Even her eldest nephew agreed to join in the hunt.

She was in the long gallery hiding a clue when she saw a coach turning into the drive.

My God! Surely not!

Alex was not due back for another three days. Where was Edward? She had not seen him all day. She must warn Alex of the danger he was in. She prayed she would not be too late. That when the time came to destroy her happiness she would have the courage to do it.

★   ★   ★

The carriage rattled along the drive and Alex viewed the relentless rain with interest. High time the crops were watered; it had been an unusually long dry spell and this was exactly the kind of weather farmers welcomed.

243

Eleanor would be pleased to see him; she did not think he was returning until after the weekend.

He would be delighted to renew his acquaintance with her nephews and niece. They had seemed to be charming children. No doubt they were causing mayhem cooped up inside, after having rampaged about in the fresh air these past few weeks. As usual, he did not alight in the front but remained until the coach reached the rear of Blakely where the carriage house and stables were situated.

Not waiting for the door to be opened by a groom, he jumped down and immediately heard childish laughter coming from inside the building. Intrigued, he went to investigate. Alexander was poking something with a stick to the delight of his small female companion.

God's teeth!

They had cornered the biggest rat he'd ever seen. 'Alexander, stop that at once.'

The child dropped his stick and threw himself into his arms. 'Papa, you have come back sooner. Mama will be so pleased to see you. Isn't this the biggest rat you've ever seen?'

Alex dropped him to the floor and turned to greet the little girl. He held out his hand and after a moment's hesitation she ran to his arms.

244

'I don't like that rat, sir, but Alexander said I should watch him, so I did.'

'Well that was very remiss of you, young man. You must take better care of young ladies and not expose them to danger. What if it had bitten her?'

Alexander grinned, unrepentant. 'Then she would have kicked me, and we would both have laughed.'

Alex chuckled; it was good to be home. 'Son, you are incorrigible. I should dust your breeches for making such a remark to your papa.'

Amanda's face paled. She must think he was serious. He gathered her close and her little body was trembling. 'Sweetheart, I was joking. Look, Alexander is not bothered, is he? I would not raise my hand to a child or a woman. Ever.' She pressed against him. When he looked up, Alexander was in the yard.

'Papa, I'm going to tell Mama you're here. Amanda, come with me.' Alex straightened, the child hanging round his neck. 'Come along, miss, I shall take you in. I think you need to wash your hands and face, don't you?'

She reached up to touch the scar that ran across his forehead, the only reminder of the injury he had received all those weeks ago. 'Does your head still pain you? When Aunt

Eleanor hit you with a stick there was so much blood, I thought you would die.'

Alex stared. 'You saw me when I was injured, Amanda?'

She smiled. 'Yes, when you were shaking Ned. Aunt Eleanor hit you on the head. Then Betty took us to the maze and I didn't see you again until we came here. I like you, you're a nice papa. I wish you were *my* papa.'

Gently Alex placed the child on her feet, giving her a little push. 'Can you find your way back in to the nursery? There's something I must do.'

The child nodded and trotted off. He was stunned. Eleanor had lied to him, he had not made improper advances. She had married him under false pretences. His stomach revolted. He turned away to cast up his accounts on a nearby carriage wheel. He finished retching and wiped his mouth on his sleeve. How could she have deceived him like this?

He had given her everything, fallen in love with her, and she had betrayed his trust. He wanted to turn round and ride away, never come back, never have to face her again. No, he couldn't do that. His children needed their father in their lives. He would not abandon them because he had lost the woman he loved. But from this moment Eleanor would be as a stranger to him.

18

Would Alex return to his apartment first, or come to seek her out? What she had to say to him should be said in privacy. He must be eager to see her or would not have returned early. She had best wait in her sitting room.

Eleanor ran the length of the long gallery, sliding to a halt on the shiny parquet floor in order to emerge like the mistress of the house and not one of the children. He would take about five minutes to reach her chambers; she had been more than that getting there herself. He should be here any moment.

She stepped into her bedchamber. Alex wasn't there. There were voices in the large dressing room where Sally and her junior sat to do the mending. She pushed open the door. The two young women looked up in surprise.

'Lord Bentley is back unexpectedly. He will be visiting me here, I wish both of you to find duties elsewhere.'

'Of course, my lady, we shall wait for you to ring before we return.'

Eleanor flushed scarlet. Never mind, better they thought she was about to tumble into bed with Alex than they knew the truth. She paused at the long mirror shaking out the creases in her dress. If she had known he was returning she would have worn something prettier than a simple sprig muslin.

Did she have time to change? No, apparel was of little importance at the moment. What was going to happen to her after she had told him? She was going to tell him the whole, everything that she had kept from him these past three months. It would be the end of her marriage, but his life was more important than her happiness.

The sitting room door crashed open. Surely that was not him? He was not one to bang doors like her brother did. She hurried in to face a man she did not know. Her beloved Alex had turned into a hard-faced stranger. He carefully closed the door, turning the key behind him with one hand.

His eyes travelled inch by inch from her head to her toes. Something wonderful died inside her. 'I have just had the most enlightening conversation with your niece, my lady. Can you guess what it might be about?'

She grabbed the back of a chair for support. She nodded; unable to answer, frozen by his arctic stare.

'You tricked me into marrying you. I made no improper advances to you. I had no need to make you an offer. You used my loss of memory to your advantage. You have broken my trust. You are a liar and I am no longer your husband.'

Tremors shook her as the blood drained from her face. It was too late to try and explain why she'd behaved as she had. He had to know about her brother's wickedness, that it was Edward's intention to murder Alex.

'Please, my lord, I know you hate me and I cannot blame you. But there is something I have to tell you.'

His eyes glittered and he shook his head. He had aged several years since she'd seen him last. 'Hate you? I could never hate you, Eleanor. I shall always love you, I'll never want another woman. However, I cannot like you anymore. I despise you for what you have done. See what you have condemned me to? Henceforth I must live like a monk, never experience the joys of intimacy. This is *your* fault. You must live with that, as I must live with your betrayal.'

He turned his back. Before she could protest, he deftly unlocked the door and vanished. She was too distressed to call him back. She should run after him and make sure he was aware of the danger that stalked Blakely Hall. How could she warn him if he wouldn't speak to her? She must find her brother, beg him to take her instead and not harm Alex.

★ ★ ★

The sound of her sobbing cut him to the quick. He wanted to return, take her in his arms and tell her it didn't matter and he forgave her. But he couldn't, honesty was more important than love. He felt wetness on his cheeks and angrily brushed it away. He could not go about in public like this; he was unmanned — knew not which way to turn. He must retire to his rooms, and find solace in a decanter of brandy.

He hesitated, disoriented by his unhappiness. Where was he going? Yes, to his apartment, no more than a few strides from the door he had left. He flung open the door to his sitting room and found Foster, grey faced, waiting there.

'My lord, I must speak urgently to you.' His man stopped, stepped forward as if to take his arm. 'My lord, you are unwell, has something happened to disturb you?'

Alex dropped into the nearest chair burying his head in his hands, fighting the urge to give in to his misery like Eleanor next door. He clenched his fists, his nails digging into his palms; the pain restored his equilibrium. He raised his face.

'Foster, she betrayed me. I didn't attack her, she attacked me. I had no need to marry her, she was not compromised but she let me believe I had behaved in the most reprehensible way. How could she have done that?'

'You don't understand my lord. She wanted to tell you, but I advised her against it.'

Alex gaped at his man. 'You knew she married me falsely?'

Foster shook his head. 'No, not at the time my lord. May I be seated? There are things I have to tell you.'

Alex listened with incredulity.

'That bastard beat my wife? Starved her? Treated her in the most appalling fashion? No wonder the poor love was so desperate to escape she grabbed my offer without question. I wish she had told me at the time, that I did not find out from a child.'

The ice around his heart dissolved. What Thorrington had done was unforgivable, inexcusable. Eleanor's sin paled to insignificance beside her brother's heinous crimes.

'Now, let me get this straight. Thorrington was behind the attack on me a few weeks ago? He wants to kill me in order to regain control of my wife's fortune? It beggars belief! The man's insane. Whatever happens to me, he can't touch her or her money. I knew what sort of man he was the moment I met him and have arranged matters accordingly.'

His despair was replaced by a fury so intense his vision clouded. 'Foster, get Thorrington's trunks packed, have his coach brought round, he will leave these premises when I've finished with him. Lady Thorrington and the children must remain here under my protection.'

Foster nodded. 'I saw Lord Thorrington by the mausoleum, sir. My lord, forgive me for saying so, but you shouldn't go alone. Please consider waiting until Tom and I are ready to accompany you.'

Alex smiled grimly. 'I don't intend to kill him. I shall give him the same treatment he gave my wife. I shall make sure everyone in Town knows him for the bastard he is. He will be received nowhere, will have to rusticate at home, or live abroad.'

Should he take his riding whip and use that instead of his fists? No, he wanted to feel the man's pain when he struck him. He took the stairs three at a time, ignoring the startled expressions of the footmen who stood permanently on guard in the Grand Hall. They jumped to open the front door. Foster was right behind him. No doubt his man had already sent word for Tom to come from the stables and join them at the mausoleum.

What in God's name is Thorrington doing there?

Alex hated the place. The crypt had been built by his great-grandfather to house the remains of the Bentley family. He never set foot in the building; the marble floors and stone effigies depressed him. He had no intention of being buried there; Anna was laid to rest in the family plot in the village churchyard. She was in the sunshine, not locked away in a dark stone vault.

He slowed his pace, gathering his thoughts, hardening his resolve. His white fury had abated somewhat to be replaced by a clinical determination to mete out the punishment the man deserved.

He rounded the corner and came face-to-face with his adversary. Not giving the man time to react, he drew back his fist and punched him with a satisfying crunch on the jaw. Alex had removed his jacket before he'd left his chamber; small wonder the footman had been startled by his appearance.

Thorrington fell backwards, blood spurting from a split lip.

'Get up, you snivelling coward, I have not finished with you yet.'

Alex saw the man react. With remarkable agility for a man who'd just been floored, he sprang to his feet with a dangerous gleam in his eyes. 'So, you know it all. Don't think it will stop here, Bentley. I shall get what is mine, one way or another.'

Alex's rage took over. He stepped in quickly, landed two smashing blows one after the other. The first broke his opponent's nose, the second blacked his eye. Thorrington staggered, recovered and aimed two feeble punches in retaliation. These were easily dodged. A few more quick jabs to the ribs and Thorrington collapsed like an empty sack.

'You hurt my wife and you hurt your children. You will not do so again or I will kill you. Do you understand me?' Each remark was punctuated by a sharp prod in the man's back. He would not demean himself by kicking him.

Thorrington was an abject, defeated man, no longer worthy of his attention. From the look of his cheek his jaw was broken. Good. Alex blew on his bruised knuckles. 'Foster, Tom, throw this object in his carriage. Make sure his coachman and valet understand they are to deliver him to his house. Failure to do so will earn my extreme displeasure.'

★　★　★

Eleanor dried her eyes on her skirt. She no longer cared what she looked like. Her life was over. The man she loved had rejected her and she didn't blame him. Foster was not at fault either for advising her not to tell Alex; this had been her decision and she must live with the consequences.

She needed to be alone, to get away from the house and not risk having to speak to the children or Jane. Where could she go? A gust of wind, and the rattle of rain on the window reminded her everyone was inside. She would venture out. Getting wet would do her no harm. There was a small garden hidden away in the grounds, behind a large beech hedge; the little summerhouse there would be ideal for her purpose.

Not bothering to collect her pelisse or put on her bonnet, she ran from the room. The footmen gaped at her disarray. She ignored them; decorum was the least of her problems. They were paid well enough to disregard what didn't concern them.

She ran through the hall and down the central passageway to the side door which led directly to the garden. She closed it quietly behind her, pausing in the stone arch to view the dismal sight of the rain lashing down. A soaking was what she deserved. If she caught a congestion of the lungs and died then it would be the Almighty's way of punishing her.

The grass underfoot was slippery, making it difficult to run, and her thin muslin skirts were soon sticking to her legs. By the time she reached the summerhouse, she was drenched to the bone. Her teeth chattered despite being inside. Inside was dry and the padded seat comfortable to curl up on. She squashed herself into the far corner, in the darkness where she wouldn't be seen. Bringing her legs up under her chin, she hugged her knees and lowered her face to touch them.

Was there anything positive to be discovered in the catastrophe that had befallen her? Foster would have told Alex about her brother by now. They would take care of matters between them. The situation was out of her hands. The water drummed on the wooden roof — her tears fell as heavily as the rain.

Perhaps there was one thing she could cling to. Alex had not said he would send her away. She could live under the same roof as him, share in the upbringing of their children. That was something. To see his dear face every day must be enough for her. The worst had not happened — he had not sent her back to live at Tendring Manor.

Her teeth clicked so loudly they could be

audible outside. She was shaking violently and couldn't think straight. To venture out dressed as she was had been a very bad idea.

★　★　★

Alex flung open the door to Eleanor's apartment. Not in there. He ran across to look in her bedchamber; that too was deserted.

Where the hell is she?

Where would she go in order to be solitary? The rain pelting against the window made him glance across the park. His heart stood still. He must be mistaken. No, Eleanor was stumbling across the grass.

What in God's name is she doing outside in such a flimsy gown? She will catch her death, she is scarcely recovered from her last bout of illness.

This was his fault; he had driven her out of the house with his rage. If anything happened to her now . . . It did not bear thinking of.

He snatched a comforter from the back of the chair, put it under his arm and raced along the corridor. He hurtled down the staircase. If he had not been so concerned, he would have laughed at the look of stupefaction on the footmen's faces. No doubt today would be a topic of conversation amongst the staff for many years to come. Their eccentric behaviour would be discussed for years.

He raced full tilt along the passage and, finding the side door unlatched, shouldered his way through to take the steps in one bound. He thundered across the grass. His boots had better purchase on the quagmire. She was going to the summerhouse. He had never disturbed her when she had disappeared in that direction several times in the early days of their marriage.

The sunken garden was almost three inches deep in water. He splashed his way through and stepped into the gloom of the small wooden building. She was shaking so violently her teeth were rattling. She had already suffered so much in her life. He had promised to protect her, not make her miserable. In two strides he was at her side.

★ ★ ★

A warm blanket was draped round Eleanor's shoulders. She inhaled the familiar scent. Alex had come for her; by some miracle, he had changed his mind. Nothing mattered now, she was safe and warm in his embrace.

'My darling, I'm so sorry. It's all over, you must forget the past. I should not have spoken to you that way, I should have waited for your explanation. Do you forgive me?'

She snuggled closer. His arms tightened. He was as wet as she. His shirt was sodden, but where was his jacket? 'Alex, you're soaking wet and in your shirtsleeves.'

She felt the rumble of his chuckle beneath her cheek. 'Of course I am, you silly goose. We are both drenched. However, *you* have a blanket around your shoulders to keep you warm.'

She reached out a hand, linking it round his neck, pulling his head down so she could see his face. The love in his eyes was unmistakable. 'Alex, I'm so sorry. Do you know about my brother as well?'

He grinned, almost cheerfully. 'I've given him a taste of his own medicine, sweetheart. He has gone, you will never be bothered by him again. And neither shall your sister and her children. They are now under my protection.'

'Did you kill him?'

His chest vibrated. 'Bloodthirsty baggage! No, I did not. I punched him several times, broke his nose, and hopefully a few ribs as well. Then I had him thrown into his coach and sent on his way. He will be a social outcast from this moment forward.'

Her shivering stopped to be replaced by a delicious warmth, an all too familiar heat spiralling down to her nether regions. How inappropriate to feel this way in the pouring rain after all that happened. Could she be considering the possibility of making love?

He kissed her gently. 'My darling, even I draw the line at being intimate in here. We should go back, have a hot bath, and then see what happens.'

She relaxed into his arms, knowing before the afternoon was over they would be skin to skin sharing an ecstasy she had not known existed until a week ago.

★ ★ ★

Eleanor suffered no ill effects from her soaking and if she had been happy before, now she was incandescent. Her burden was gone. Alex knew everything there was to know about her. She had told him of the wretched life she had been obliged to live until he had saved her. They heard no more from her brother. Jane was also free of the degradation she had been suffering at Edward's hands these past few years.

The house was full of laughter, and plans for Alexander's birthday party the following week were progressing wonderfully. She and Alex decided to invite the villagers as they were owed a party after the one that had been cancelled.

There were seven children in residence, enough to make up a Blakely Hall team for all the races. The errant governess finally arrived and Eleanor was happy to give Miss Smithson a chance to demonstrate her prowess with her own children. It would be a relief not to have the nuisance of searching herself. The young woman was far younger than Eleanor had anticipated. The plain lilac gown did not disguise the woman's curves. With her golden curls arranged prettily on the crown of her head, she looked nothing like a governess.

Eleanor greeted the new arrival warmly. As long as the girl was efficient and the children liked her then that was what mattered, after all.

The night before the party, she lay in Alex's arms after a particularly passionate episode. 'I am so looking forward to tomorrow, my love. Everything has changed for us. I am free to be happy for the first time in years. Are you happy too?'

He smoothed back her hair, kissing the corner of her mouth tenderly. 'I thought I had showed you several times, my darling, just how happy I am to be with you.'

She giggled. 'That is another matter, my lord. I'm talking about there being seven children, a governess, a nanny and five nursery maids, plus my sister-in-law happily established in the east wing. You *know* everything has changed.'

'Ned told me how things have been since

you left. He's a brave young man. I have decided he and Jonathan shall not go to their father's old school. I have cancelled their places. They shall go to Felsted, where I went, instead. They can join after Christmas. This term they shall have free to recover from their ill treatment. They can do lessons with the governess.'

She yawned. 'Strange, don't you think, that Miss Smithson took so long to arrive here? One would think toothache a small thing to keep her from her duties. Why should she wish to remain at Thorrington Manor with my brother? Well, she is here now, and I think her an excellent choice.'

'Possibly, my love, Thorrington wouldn't allow her to leave until she had the where-withal sent to her. Did I tell you I have sent letters everywhere? He will be blackballed at White's. I expect he has gone abroad. He could catch a package from Harwich, could he not?'

He gathered her close to his side, putting his naked thigh across hers. 'Sweetheart, that is quite enough conversation. I need some sleep. You have exhausted me tonight.'

'Nonsense, the fight with my brother last week fatigued you.'

Having the last word on the discussion, she lapsed into a contented silence.

19

The day dawned with clear blue skies and not a trace of the rain that had marred everyone's enjoyment recently. Alex propped himself on one elbow and watched Eleanor flinging open the shutters and exclaiming in delight.

'My darling girl, how many times do I have to tell you it's not your job to open the shutters? Why do I pay such an exorbitant amount of money to my staff if you are to do their jobs for them?'

She grinned. 'If you returned to your chamber as you ought to do, my dear Alex, then you would not know whether I open them or not.'

'*Touché*! I have decided I'm never sleeping alone again, I want you to move into my apartment immediately.' He smiled. 'However, it will be in order for you to have these rooms to use when I'm away.'

'I may keep my apartment? Am I not allowed to remain in the lord and master's bed in his absence? How kind of you, my lord. Do I have your permission to use my own closets as well?' She clapped her hands like a child then tossed her head, accompanying this with a withering glance.

His eyes narrowed and his lips twitched. Without answering he swung out of bed striding toward her unashamedly naked. The shock on her face made his gesture worth it.

★ ★ ★

'Alex, you must not walk around like that; my abigail might come in at any moment. *She* would die from shock and *you* of mortification.'

He continued to approach, a slight smile playing around his mobile mouth. She realized too late his intent. With a squeak, she attempted to dodge under his arm but he caught a handful of her hair which was flowing loose around shoulders.

'I have you now, little baggage. I have a mind to carry you through to my apartment this minute.'

He would not risk it; she would call his bluff. When she tumbled into his arms, his heat burnt through the thin cloth of her nightgown.

'You're my husband and I your obedient servant. I would not dream of arguing.'

He grabbed her, one arm under her knees the other around her shoulders. Still without a word being spoken, he strode boldly across the carpet toward the communicating door. When he removed one hand to open the door, he kept her where she was by pressing her against the wall in a most undignified manner.

'Put me down at once, Alex. I have no wish . . . '

Her voice stuttered to a halt as they came face to face with Foster, who was attending to the curtains. She buried her face in Alex's shoulder, knowing she was pink from nose to toes.

With commendable aplomb, Foster bowed. 'Good morning, my lord, my lady. It's a fine day for the party.'

Party? How could he talk of something so mundane when she was in her nightgown and her husband in nothing at all?

She kept her face hidden until the door closed. They were alone in the room. 'Alex, how could you? I shall never look him in the eye again without embarrassment.'

'This is entirely your fault, sweetheart. Foster is not bothered that I am unclothed, and I can assure you his eyes were firmly averted at all times.' He chuckled and in two quick steps tossed her as if she was a pillow into the centre of his massive tester bed. She scarcely had time to draw breath before he arrived beside her. Foster was immediately forgotten.

Considerably later than usual, they appeared in the breakfast parlour.

Jane looked up from her breakfast. 'Good morning, Lord Bentley, Eleanor. It's rare that I am here before you.'

Eleanor blushed. 'Good morning, Jane. Are the children excited about today? Have you been up to the nursery this morning?' If she had asked this question a few months ago the answer would have been a definite no.

Jane nodded. 'I have indeed, it's little short of pandemonium up there. Even Ned has deigned to become involved. He insists that as the eldest, he has the right to draw up the list of races. Of course, Jonathan and Peter disagree. It will all end in tears long before the party starts.'

They sat for some minutes in companionable silence, munching their way through a substantial breakfast. Eleanor found she had a prodigious appetite at the moment.

The village folk and their children were to arrive at one o'clock. The first race was to start promptly at thirty minutes past the hour.

'Miss Smithson will, no doubt, soon have them all in order. She's a treasure, Jane. You have saved me the bother of employing a reliable governess myself. I am so pleased you're making your home with us, this house is far too big for one family.' Eleanor wiped her mouth on her napkin.

'And the hundred staff, my love, pray do not forget them, I beg you. I am well served, but quite ruined.'

'That's true, Alex. However, I think it quite ridiculous we require so many servants. Could we not perhaps close down half the house and reduce the number?'

'What would happen to them if I did, Eleanor? My role is to provide employment for as many of my people as possible. I also support those facing difficulties in whatever way I can. I have been neglecting my duties shamefully these past few years but that has changed now.'

'Of course, Alex. Far better they are gainfully employed than living on charity. By the bye, have you seen Ned flying his falcon? He's quite the expert, you know. He shall give a demonstration this afternoon, I cannot believe he has been able to learn such a complex skill so quickly.'

Jane smiled proudly. 'He's a quick study, Eleanor. But if I'm honest, I believe the falconer has given him a fully trained bird to handle. He just has to do the right things in the correct order and the peregrine responds.'

Alex rose. 'Pray excuse me, ladies, but I

must oversee the setting up of the trestles in the park, and that the ale, brewed specially for today, has been transferred safely.

Eleanor called after him. 'How many villagers and children are expected this afternoon?'

He glanced over his shoulder and raised an eyebrow, his lopsided smile sending heat waves through her body. He was always reminding her not to shout as it was unladylike. She knew that perfectly well, but after living repressed and miserable for years under her brother's control she felt like a young girl again, not a mature woman of almost five and twenty.

That very morning she had attempted to slide down the banister and he had physically removed her, playfully threatening to put her over his knee if she attempted such an idiotic scheme again. She widened her eyes; his darkened in response.

'You are temptation incarnate, my love. Leave me be, I beg you I have more important things to do.' She heard him laughing as he walked away.

Jane was decidedly put out. 'You two should be ashamed of yourselves, behaving in such a manner when you're around each other. I shudder to think what the staff make of it all.'

'I have no idea, Jane. No, that's incorrect. I'm certain they're glad we are so happy. I don't give a fig for propriety. We don't stand on ceremony here. It might be a grand house, but it's our home and we shall do as we please when we're here.'

Jane sniffed and changed the subject. 'I cannot imagine that Lord Bentley is needed outside for such a mundane task, my dear. Do you think we drove him away with our chatter?'

'I am certain of it, Jane. I intend to leave everything pertaining to outside matters to Foster; he is far more capable than I. Unfortunately I must go and speak to the housekeeper. That *is* my duty.'

'Good heavens, Eleanor. I would have thought you would revel in the responsibility of running this grand house.'

'I would do so, indeed, were it not for the fact that she is far more efficient than I could ever be at the task. Why should I interfere for the sake of doing so? At the moment I'm content to drift in a sea of idleness, devoting all my time to my husband and children.'

★ ★ ★

Eleanor appeared a few minutes past the appointed hour to greet the villagers. All

269

seven children, their governess, Betty and Daisy, plus Alex and Jane were already there. She was tardy, but it had been worth it. The party would be her first formal appearance as lady of the manor; she wanted Alex to be proud.

Her fine silk gown of damask rose had small pleated sleeves and little roses sewn around the neckline. The garment was a recreation of her wedding dress. Her skirts hung gracefully from the high waist, swirling about her feet, upon which she wore matching slippers with identical roses embroidered on the toes. Her hair was arranged with deep pink ribbons, the exact same shade as the sash tied prettily to one side.

Alex turned. He had no need for words, his expression said it all. He stopped in mid-sentence and walked to meet her. He held out his hand and she placed hers in it. He closed his fingers.

'You look *ravissante*, my love. Every inch the mistress of Blakely. I cannot believe you're the same woman I saw playing cricket a few months ago.'

'Thank you, I think. I have put on weight recently. I lost so much over these past few years. I appear to have filled out in all the necessary areas.'

His hand tightened and he whispered in

her ear. 'Behave yourself, sweetheart, or I shall be forced to take drastic action. I believe our guests might be somewhat startled if I were to do so.'

In perfect harmony with him, she stood at his side to greet the flock of village folk who were hurrying across the grass. The shouts and cries of the children as they saw the treats in store for them added to the air of gaiety. The magnificent iced cake, the centrepiece of the tea, was pointed to in awe. She believed she was excited as they to be attending her first real party.

★　★　★

'What is wrong, Miss Smithson?' Eleanor moved away from her sister-in-law in answer to the urgent gesture from the governess.

'Lord Edward has had an accident, my lady, and does not wish Lady Thorrington to know. He has asked for you to come.'

'Is it serious? I cannot keep it from his mother if it is.'

'No, my lady. More embarrassing than dangerous, which is why he wishes it to be you who helps him.'

Eleanor watched Alex pick up two squabbling children, holding them apart and laughing down at their red faces. The argument appeared to be over the rosette awarded to the winner of the race.

He was so good with children, so good with everyone. He was the kindest, dearest man in the whole world. And he was hers.

'I shall come at once, Miss Smithson. I am relieved it's nothing to worry about. It would be a shame to spoil the party; the event has been such a success don't you think?' The governess was already out of earshot, hurrying back toward the house, but instead of going in, she veered left and headed through the shrubbery.

Eleanor dashed after her. Why was she in such a rush if Ned was not seriously harmed? She hesitated, glancing back at Alex. Should she send a message to him just in case he was needed? Miss Smithson gestured for her to hurry. She would investigate first and send for reinforcements if necessary.

'Miss Smithson, what has Lord Edward done? Where is he? I don't recognize this part of the garden.'

'He didn't wish me to tell you, my lady. Lord Edward was most insistent on that point. We are almost there, he will be most grateful that you have come unaccompanied.'

The young woman said no more and was obviously embarrassed herself, so Eleanor decided to question her no further. This part of the formal garden was quiet; the noise from the children seemed a long way away. Where were they going? Over the clipped hedges she saw the domed roof of the hideous mausoleum. She always avoided it and had no wish to view the buried remains of Alex's ancestors.

A crypt — exactly the sort of place a curious boy might wish to investigate. Although why Ned had decided to do so when there was so much excitement going on elsewhere, she had no idea. The governess did not pause, but raced up the steps and through the door which had been left ajar. Breathless from her run, Eleanor followed the governess, expecting it to be light, that Miss Smithson would have thought to provide Ned with a candle.

She could see nothing, suffocating blackness closed in, the only illumination the sunlight from the opened door. Where was he? For that matter where was Miss Smithson? She couldn't see either of them, couldn't hear a sound. Then a hand was rammed between her shoulder blades and she was flying forwards. She landed painfully on her knees. By the time she scrambled up the door had slammed, leaving her in total darkness in a building full of dead people.

'Tell me, Foster, was that the last race? I fear my nerves could not stand another altercation between the losers.'

'I think that was the last, my lord. The rosettes have been presented, the children have their prizes. Look, they are all going over to the trestles to attack the food laid out there. Your part is done, sir.'

'Thank the good Lord for that! I shall make my escape.' Alex looked around. Where was Eleanor amongst the crowd? Their children along with her nephews and nieces were easily spotted amongst the more plainly dressed village children. No, young Ned was missing.

She was the only one wearing pink. She should be easy to see even among so many. He stood well over two yards in his stockings, able to see over most people's heads.

He scanned the masses and felt a moment of unease; Eleanor was not there.

She must be inside, or had gone with Ned somewhere. There was no need to be concerned, but it would set his mind at rest to ask Lady Thorrington if she knew where either of them were. She was talking earnestly to the second of her sons, Jonathan.

'Lady Thorrington, excuse me for interrupting, but have you any idea where Eleanor is? I cannot see her here.'

'I don't know, my lord.' She frowned. 'In fact, I don't believe I have seen her for some time. Jonathan, when did you last see your Aunt Eleanor?'

'About an hour ago, Mama. Miss Smithson came over to speak to her and they went inside together. Shall I go and see?'

Alex stopped him. 'That will not be necessary, young man, but thank you for your offer. Go and get something to eat before the others finish it. I intended to go inside anyway. I need a drink of something stronger than lemonade.'

Foster caught up with him as he was crossing the dry moat. 'Would you like me to make discreet enquiries as to her ladyship's whereabouts, my lord?'

'Yes, do that. I should try the falconry; I think she is with Lord Edward.'

The butler approached him in the hall with a silver tray upon which rested a letter.

'Where did that come from? I didn't see any post delivered this afternoon.'

'The note was brought by hand, sir, I have no notion by whom. I only discovered it a moment ago. The item cannot have been there long, my lord.'

Alex didn't recognize the writing No doubt it was from one of his tenants. He would read it later. He tucked it in his jacket pocket and forgot about it. He asked for coffee and brandy to be sent to him in his study.

An hour later, the sound of revelry continued unabated outside. He supposed he must reappear at some point. He turned to collect the jacket which he had discarded earlier and noticed the paper. He might as well read it in case it required a response of some sort. He opened the note and his fingers clenched.

I have Lady Eleanor.
Do not bring anyone with you or she will die.
Come at once to the mausoleum.

Written in well-formed letters, the letter was obviously the work of someone tutored. The missive wasn't signed. There was no need. He knew who it was from. Thorrington had taken Eleanor.

God's Teeth!

This had been sitting in his pocket for over an hour. Would whoever it was think he had ignored it, and harm Eleanor? A sharp rap on the door disturbed his thoughts.

Foster stepped in, followed by Tom. They had not waited to be invited to enter. 'My lord, Lady Eleanor is nowhere to be found. We have searched everywhere apart from the house; we did not wish to alarm anyone inside.'

Alex schooled his features into nonchalance, slipping the paper out of sight before it could be commented on. Foster had seen, and was looking at him curiously.

'Nothing of importance — a query from a tenant, I shall deal with it later. Lady Eleanor had a headache and is lying down in her room. I'm sorry, I should have sent word to you.' Somehow he kept his tone light. 'Go out and enjoy yourselves, there is free ale and you will be needed to join the tug of war. I thank you for your assistance. I'm going to check how she is and then I shall join you outside.'

Foster grinned. 'We're enjoying it, my lord. It's far too long since there was anything of this sort held at Blakely. Do you wish me to return to your chamber when you change for dinner?'

'There is to be no dinner tonight. A cold collation does not require anyone to dress formally.' His mind was already elsewhere. He wanted to race from the house. Her life might depend on his actions during these next crucial minutes. He was being watched; someone on his staff must be in the pay of that madman. He must not act precipitously.

As soon as the door closed behind his men, he was able to move. His breathing was laboured and his hands clammy. There was a knife tucked into his boot top, would this be enough? It had stood him in good stead when out riding on more than one occasion. Should he risk secreting a small duelling pistol in his pocket?

There was one in his desk. He glanced around nervously, almost expecting to see a servant lurking in the shadows. The room, of course, was empty. It took him moments to snatch the powder pouch and find the shot. He primed and loaded the pistol then popped it into his jacket pocket, patting his coat to check there was no tell-tale bulge.

The corridor was empty. For once no footman was waiting outside to run errands. He closed the door silently and walked soft-footed through the house, taking a less frequented route leading to a rear door. The sounds of merriment continued at the front of the house. How was it possible he was in the middle of this nightmare when everyone else was celebrating?

As he made his way through the formal garden to the mausoleum, he realized why Thorrington had chosen this place. The man had been beaten into submission, humiliated by him, right here. Thorrington would want to take his revenge. He cursed the fact that he had underestimated the man's capacity for evil.

From the corner of his eye he saw a

movement, a flash of skirt. He looked again but there was nothing. Was it possible the traitor in his home was female? He paused on the edge of the gravel square that fronted the hideous marble building. There was no sign of anyone, no footprints in the gravel — all was silent as a tomb.

He knew who had delivered the letter, who had been watching him — the governess, Miss Smithson. Eleanor had left the party with her; the woman must have enticed her away somehow. This must mean Thorrington hadn't arrived. Alex was being led into the same trap as Eleanor. This didn't stop him moving forward.

He walked slowly on to the open space, his shoulders twitching. One of the riflemen could drop him in his tracks.

20

Alex approached the mausoleum, alert for any sound that might herald an attack. The door was closed. Well, that was to be expected. The key had been left in the lock. He was obviously intended to go in. He didn't hesitate; whatever fate awaited him, Eleanor was inside in the dark on her own and he wished to be beside her.

This was Thorrington's work. This time the bastard wouldn't get away with it. Alex was not a violent man, but when he came face-to-face with Thorrington, the man would not live to see another dawn. Not if he had harmed a single hair of his beloved's head.

Alex unlocked the door, the noise harsh in the eerie silence that surrounded him. Remaining in the opening for a moment, he strained his ears, but all was silent. Then there was a whimper in the darkness.

'Eleanor, sweetheart, is that you? Are you hurt?'

'Alex, you shouldn't have come. This is a trick; it's you they want. I'm cold and uncomfortable, but not harmed.' She stifled a sob. 'Please go away, wait outside, there's no one in here who can hurt me. You will be safer where you can see what's happening. Miss Smithson is a wicked woman, she lured me here. I have no idea why she's involved in my brother's evil machinations.'

He stood, allowing his eyes to adjust to the darkness. As soon as he stepped away from the door it would be slammed and he, too, would be helpless in the dark. Eleanor was right, much more sensible to remain where he could apprehend Thorrington when he arrived. Sensible it might be; but she mustn't be alone in this horrible place a moment longer.

'Let me think, my love; if I'm only dealing with a woman then it must be safe for you to come to me. When I move away from the door the same thing will happen; I shall be locked in with you. I guessed the governess was behind the note. She must be under the thrall of your brother.'

Her voice sounded stronger. 'I'm all right now I know you're close. I can see you framed in the sunlight. If you stay where you are, I'll get up and walk to you'

Keeping alert for a possible attack from the rear, he waited for his brave love to approach. 'Keep talking and walking; I shall guide you.' From the darkness she appeared, her lovely gown covered in dirt and her hair escaping

281

from its ribbons. He held out his hand. 'Not far to go, my love. Be strong, keep moving forwards.'

Things were going to be all right. Perhaps he had been mistaken, this was no more than an unpleasant practical joke. She was at the end of the shaft of sunlight. She screamed a warning. Too late. Something sharp smashed between his shoulders, catapulting him forwards.

His moment's inattention had given Smithson the opportunity she needed. The pain in his back intensified. He had failed. Then the world went black.

* * *

'Alex, my love, what has she done to you? Alex, speak to me.' She dropped to her knees and inched her way to where he'd fallen. The image of Miss Smithson's face as she plunged the pitchfork into his back would live with her forever. Had that wicked woman killed him? Had the prongs punctured his heart?

A strong, warm hand reached out and grabbed her knee. 'I'm not badly hurt, my darling. More stunned than anything. For a horrible moment, when it went dark, I thought I was done for.'

Was he grinning in the darkness? He

sounded almost gleeful. 'Alex, she pushed the pitchfork right into you. Are you sure you're not bleeding?'

He slid toward her, then she was in his arms and her fear vanished. 'I think I have a couple of puncture holes, but the prongs didn't go in far. I shan't bleed to death if that's what you fear. However, if we remain kneeling on this icy floor we shall certainly *freeze* to death. We must get up and find our way to one of the tombs. We can sit on that.'

'We can't move about in here. I spent an age to find the wall in order to lean against it.' The last thing she wanted to do was sit on a dead body. 'I don't think I can walk anywhere, I'm too frightened to move. We know where the door is, do we have to leave it?'

'Close your eyes. It's easier to move about when you have made the blackness your choice. Your brain will believe you to be playing a game of blindman's buff.'

He pulled her up, and then with his arm firmly around her waist he guided her confidently across the slippery marble floor. Her breathing steadied. She was safe. She was sure sitting on the marble tomb would be no warmer than being seated on the floor. She guessed why he had suggested this.

'You think we should hide, that we shall be

safer there when my brother comes to find us?'

His arm tightened. 'Good girl, you understand exactly. Your brother must be deranged and means to kill us both. He can hardly lock us in here and expect to get away with it.'

'We both saw the Smithson woman; she must know we will identify her, that her punishment will be transportation at the very least.'

'Stand still, my love. If my calculations are correct, we must be almost there. I don't wish to cause myself or you further damage by colliding with an effigy. Walk behind me, darling, hold on to my jacket. Then if I stumble you won't come down as well.'

They shuffled forward until he swore as his toe struck the tomb. 'Excellent! Let me see, I should be able to tell exactly where we are when I identify this statuary.'

He was fumbling about in front of her. 'Yes, it's my great-grandfather's vault. I have our exact position. We are at the far right-hand side of the building about three yards from the exterior wall. There's space where we can hide. We will be invisible to anyone looking from the doorway. I doubt even with a lantern it will be possible to see where we are.'

* ★ *

This predicament was entirely down to his stupidity. He should have moved back from the doorway as soon as he knew Eleanor was safe. Now they were both at risk. But no, he couldn't have left her by herself. He would do the same again given the choice. What he should have done was bring both his pistols, but it was too late to repine. He must make do with what he had.

Should he tell her he had a gun in his pocket, with which he was intending to shoot whoever came to find them? The range of his duelling pistol was not sufficient to fire from cover. He would let Thorrington get close before discharging his weapon. He was a good shot and there would be only one chance. He would not need a second one.

'Foster knows that you're missing, sweetheart. He saw me read the note; I'm sure he will realize the significance of the letter and link it to our disappearance. He will come looking soon.'

'Why should he look here? Nobody ever comes to this horrible building; it's such a depressing place. We could be here for days and no one the wiser.'

She was far too quick. He'd hoped this would not occur to her, at least not initially.

285

Should he reassure her that they would be discovered before they starved to death, or remind her that something far more deadly might well appear this very night?

'Well, we must wait until someone does come, either friend or foe. Whatever happens, I promise I'll let no one harm you.'

This was not the time to tell her that he intended to kill her brother.

★ ★ ★

Thorrington slumped in his coach, waiting for dark to fall. If Helen did as they had arranged, both Eleanor and Bentley would now be incarcerated in the mausoleum. He was glad their last hours would be spent in such a place. He intended to approach from the tradesmen's entrance — no one would be looking there. This was not his usual carriage, nor his usual coachmen. These were men employed at great expense, men who would turn a blind eye and a deaf ear to anything that happened.

His jaw hurt like the very devil. He was sure it had been fractured when that bastard had attacked him. His right eye was still swollen and his nose would heal with a crook in it. He'd been living on slops since the fight. Breathing sent stabs of agony through his chest. He would never get his hands on Eleanor's money; his lawyers had explained it to him.

Tonight was for revenge.

Helen Smithson was eager and willing in bed, unlike his frigid wife. She had the idea that she apply for the position as governess to his children. She was well-educated, a gentle woman fallen on hard times when he had made her his mistress.

He had written her references himself, knowing she would give all the answers his wife required. Having her living under his own roof had made the waiting these past few weeks much easier.

When Jane requested Helen join her at Blakely Hall, it had been a godsend. He now had a spy in the enemy's camp, someone who would do his bidding without a second thought.

A gust of wind rocked the carriage and he smiled. Bentley and Eleanor would have been missed by now, they would be searching throughout the grounds. No doubt Helen would be wailing and weeping like the rest of them. But they would never look in the mausoleum. He had discovered the where-abouts of the key on his visit here, had been intrigued by the building. At the time he hadn't realized how significant his inside knowledge would be.

The moon was no more than a sliver of silver in the sky; he pulled his beaver low over his eyes, turned up the collar of his cape and rapped on the roof of the carriage. This was the signal for the coachmen to move. The horses' hooves were wrapped in rags, there were no lanterns on the coach and the two men on the box had their faces muffled in dark cloths. They had walked the route, knew exactly where they were going and could do so without benefit of extra light.

He had perfected his scheme. Bentley and Eleanor were to be suffocated, that way when their bodies were eventually discovered it would be thought they had died from natural causes. It would be a double tragedy. His heart pounded and he flinched. It was just possible he might gain financially somehow from their deaths, but he was fairly sure that bastard would have tied up Eleanor's money in such a way it would never return to its rightful place.

Jane, however, would be forced to return to him, and he could get his revenge on her and the children for deserting him. He closed his eyes, visualizing the scene, the part he would play when the bodies were discovered. He would offer his condolences, and as the only male relative of the Bentley brats there was a remote chance he could become their guardian. Then he could move to Blakely Hall and live in luxury at someone else's expense.

He shrugged, wincing as his ribs protested. Whatever the outcome, he would celebrate the fact that they were dead, that he had been the instrument in their demise. No one would suspect him. He would return unseen to Tendring Manor and his staff would swear he had been in his house the entire time.

★   ★   ★

'Alex, I need to relieve myself. It has been hours, and I cannot wait another moment.'

'In which case, sweetheart, let me guide you to a suitable corner. I promise I shall not see a thing.'

If she was not so cold she would have laughed. 'We have done some extraordinary things together, have we not? Although I much preferred what we did in the charcoal burner's house, to being obliged to relieve ourselves on the remains of your ancestors.'

He chuckled, the sound echoing strangely around the building, giving her a much-needed boost to her confidence. Botheration! The hem of her dress was wet. That was insignificant compared to all the indignities she had suffered today. He held out his hand and guided her back to their hiding place.

'Pray excuse me, my darling, I must follow your example.'

The splashing in the darkness made her smile, it was so much easier for a man to accomplish these things standing up. Beside her in moments, he crouched in the corner again, his back hard against the wall, the marble tomb protecting them.

'Sit down, sweetheart. This is the only enjoyable part of our experience.'

She snuggled into his lap, enfolded tenderly within his embrace. They had been whiling away the time asking each other riddles, talking about the children, the future. If anything was going to happen, it could be at any moment.

'How long have we been here, Alex?'

'Several hours. I have tried to keep a mental check. I believe it could be as late as nine o'clock.'

'Jane and the children will be so worried. If nothing happens tonight, then we will know it is my brother's intention to leave us here to starve.'

'It will not come to that. Foster will search this place eventually.'

His hold tightened and she tilted her face to receive a gentle kiss. There was something she needed to know, and she would not have dared to ask in any other circumstances.

'Alex, tell me, what was Anna like?' She thought him offended, the tension in his body was palpable. He sighed.

'She was nothing like you. Anna was small and blonde and gloriously rounded. She came out in Society the same season I did. That was when we met. It was love at first sight for both of us. My father was alive then, although ailing. My mama and two younger sisters were killed in a carriage accident when I was twelve.'

'How dreadful! I had no idea your family died in such a tragic way.'

'Anna was the only child of doting parents; they were delighted she wished to marry me. We were both so young, I was scarcely eighteen when I met her, and had not reached my majority when we married. She, the same age as I.'

Eleanor wished she had known him then, but she would have been in the schoolroom.

'My father died soon after. Fortunately I was one and twenty and was able to take over the estates without the need of a guardianship. Somehow Anna and I learnt the secret of the marriage bed together. I admit it was some time before we both enjoyed it.'

Eleanor was not sure he should be

discussing such things with her, but he was engrossed in his memories, hardly aware of her at all.

'A year and a half after our wedding, Lucy was born. Her birth was a perfect moment to hold the product of our love in my arms. We were so happy. However, Anna was with child again immediately, Elizabeth is only eleven months younger than Lucy. Alexander arrived two years later.'

'You were young to have so much responsibility.'

He ignored her comment, lost in his reminiscences. 'I could not keep away from her. She had been told that nursing the baby herself would prevent her from conceiving. This is a fallacy, at least in our case it was.' He swallowed.

'Please, darling, don't continue if it distresses you.'

'No, you should know everything. You are my wife now. The last pregnancy was fraught with difficulty and Anna went into labour prematurely. Both she and the baby died.'

'I'm so sorry. That must have been an awful time for you.' His embrace tightened and she reached round to stroke his cheek.

'I was heartbroken. Alexander was a few months old, Elizabeth three, Lucy not even four. I abandoned them and moved into my townhouse. I could not accept her death. I almost killed myself with drink, went down rarely to visit, left them in the clutches of that dreadful nanny. I should be horsewhipped for my neglect.'

'My darling, you must not blame yourself. Grief does strange things to people. How did you recover? What saved you?'

He didn't answer immediately, then laughed ruefully. 'I met a beautiful widow, she became my mistress. Sarah saved my life. I shall always be in debt to her.

'And I too. Had she not stepped in, your children would be as orphans and I would not have met you. Do you still see her?'

'God! Of course not. I wrote to her and told her that our liaison was over and thanked her for her good advice. I also wished her well.'

'Whatever do you mean?'

'Sarah told me to look for a complaisant wife; she said I would not be happy until my children were properly taken care of. My intention was to marry someone who would make no demands on me and then to live the life I wanted in Town.'

She was about to answer when he stiffened his hand on her lips as warning. He had heard something. Sure enough, there was a slight scrape as the key was turned in the lock. Silently he lifted her from his lap, placing her in the corner away from danger. He had already told her whatever happened she must remain where she was.

He was rummaging in his pocket. There was a loud click. He was cocking a pistol.

He was armed. Thank God! Perhaps they did have a chance of escaping with their lives.

21

Edward crept two yards behind his minions. They smelt rank as did most of their kind. As long as they did what he wanted, he would be satisfied. He had no intention of committing the murder personally. He was quite prepared to shoot either of them, but putting a pillow over a face, pressing down whilst legs and arms flailed helplessly? He hadn't the stomach for that.

The man in front gripped the key. It grated noisily in the lock. Edward cursed silently. Would the noise have alerted Bentley? The lanterns they were carrying were blacked out on three sides like the ones the smugglers used. The lit side was facing him, the glow falling inside his cape. He dare not risk a glimmer showing in the darkness and alerting any searchers.

The door inched open. He peered over the shoulders of the two men. The darkness was impenetrable, totally silent. No pleading, no shuffling, no noise at all.

Dammit to hell! Where are they?

He didn't fancy shuffling around the mausoleum. Bentley was dangerous; his fists could do damage if he managed to spring out on them.

They were three to one; the odds were in his favour. He edged his way forward. With the light inside his cloak he could only see his feet. Anyone else would be hard put to benefit. He stopped dead as something occurred to him. That bastard Bentley was armed.

'He's got a gun,' he whispered.

The man in front froze, his companion cannoned into him and fell backwards. Edward dropped his lantern. It tipped open and the flame caught the corner of his cloak. Before he could douse it, he was on fire. The pain in his legs was excruciating. He tore at the fastening and, wrenching it free, threw it away from him.

★ ★ ★

The door was opening slowly. Alex moved forward, crouching low, waiting to see his target. From the sound, there was more than one man to deal with. Kill the leader, and the others would make a run for it.

The lantern light glimmered on the floor. After the pitch darkness, the light was enough for him to see they were coming in his direction. Then the two men in front halted,

Thorrington stumbled and somehow his lantern set fire to his cloak.

Alex levelled his pistol. He guessed what would happen next. When the cloak was flung in a fiery arc it illuminated his target bright as day. With icy calm he aimed, and pulled the trigger. Thorrington reeled backwards, crashing to the marble floor. Alex reached down and removed the stiletto from his boot. There was no time to reload his gun.

The two ruffians who had accompanied Thorrington seemed undecided, then surged forward, deciding to finish the job. They couldn't afford to be identified. There was no chance of taking both of them, but he would do his damnedest. With the door wide open there was a chance the noise of the attack would be heard, sound travelled further at night.

'Scream, Eleanor, scream as loud as you can. Whatever happens, don't stop — our lives depend on it.'

Before he was ready, she began. The noise split the air so horribly that if he had not known it was her he would have been terrified. The din was enough to distract the first man. Alex dived in the darkness, kicking out the man's feet from under him and sending his pistol skittering across the marble floor. He had no wish to kill again, but would if he had to. He had the man around the throat, his knife pressing into his neck. 'Tell your friend to drop his gun, or you're a dead man.'

The man grunted. 'Save yourself, Davie. Kill the cove; if we're taken we're done for anyway.'

Alex had no choice, he plunged his knife into the man's neck, dropping with the corpse to the floor in the hope this would confuse his opponent. He would make a smaller target crouched as he was. He was too far away to reach the remaining man. The mausoleum still echoed with unearthly screams. He had seconds to live, and sent up a fervent prayer for deliverance.

Running feet on the gravel alerted him. Someone had heard Eleanor. A small figure exploded into the mayhem and launched himself on the back of the remaining villain. The man's pistol exploded harmlessly, the bullet ricocheting off a nearby tomb. Alex was on his feet, his blood-stained knife at the man's throat before he could move.

'Ned, you saved my life. Well done, my boy. Let me have him now.'

The boy remained firmly attached to the man's back. For a moment Alex was too shaken to move. The screaming continued, unabated. 'Stop, sweetheart, it's over. We're safe.'

Thankfully the noise ceased. Then others were around him. Ned was lifted from the stinking man and rough hands took the villain's arms, dragging him away to lock him up. The mausoleum was unexpectedly full of light. He dropped his knife and wiped his blood-stained hands on his breeches.

Eleanor hurtled across the floor, launching herself into his arms, sobbing wildly. 'I thought he killed you, Alex, I was so scared. I love you so much. Is it finally over?'

He lifted her, pressing her shaking body against his. 'Yes, my darling, it's done. Let me take you away from here, you're freezing. Plenty of time for talking later.'

★ ★ ★

The body of her brother on the floor caused her no regret. She snuggled into Alex, thanking God for sparing them both. Now was not the time to consider the ramifications, how things must be arranged to avoid a scandal. Such thoughts must be left until she was warm again.

She kept her face pressed into his shoulder as he bounded upstairs and along to his own apartment. He walked straight to the bedchamber, placing her tenderly in the centre of his bed. To her astonishment he grabbed the front of her gown and ripped it in two, tossing the pieces to one side, leaving her in her undergarments.

'There, my love, those are relatively clean and dry. Get under the covers. There are things I have to do; I shall join you as soon as I can. I will send your girl to attend to you.'

He hurried off. She wished he had stayed. As soon as he left the room, her teeth started chattering. Whether from shock or cold she had no notion. She had been a veritable castanet these past few weeks. She thought she might be shaken apart by the tremors that rocked her.

Then Jane was there, and Sally. 'My dear girl, what a dreadful business. Come, there's a bath drawn in Bentley's dressing room for him, yours is waiting in your own chambers. But as you are here, you might as well use his.'

Part lifted, part guided by the two women, Eleanor arrived in his dressing room. There, they removed her undergarments and helped her to step into the bath. This was far bigger than her own, made to accommodate a man. The water was not hot, but warm enough to wash away the grime. The bath restored her equilibrium after the hours spent in that vile place. However, it was not hot enough to linger. A voluminous nightshirt was dropped over her head; she looked at it in astonishment.

Jane laughed. 'Well, my dear, if you will come to your husband's apartments, rather than your own, you must make do with what's available.'

The bedroom was ablaze with candlelight; two maids rubbed warming pans between the sheets. Eleanor stretched out with a sigh of pleasure. Then her delight in the moment faded. 'Jane, I have some painful news for you.'

'There's no need to tell me, my dear. My husband is dead, and I'm glad of it. My son is the Earl of Tendring. There is only one Edward Thorrington now. And *he* is a hero.'

A deep voice echoed her remark. 'Indeed he is, my lady. He saved our lives with his bravery. He is nothing like his father. I believe your husband was deranged.' He smiled at Eleanor and her insides melted. 'Lady Thorrington, everything has been arranged in order to avoid a scandal. The governess was your husband's mistress. It will be said he was a victim of a lover's quarrel. It makes no matter, the girl will hang anyway. Better it is thought he was a philanderer than a murderer.'

'Thank you, sir. I don't care who knows about my husband as long as my children are safe. I'm glad there will be no gossip. I don't blame you in the slightest for shooting him. I would have done the same myself if I'd been there. I shall return to my own home immediately. I'm hoping you will still stand guardian to my children.'

'I would be honoured, my lady. Please, do not rush off on our account. We are happy to have you here; stay, at least until the dust settles.'

She smiled and nodded. 'Thank you, I should be glad to. It's late, we should all have been abed long ago. I will see you in the morning.'

The bedroom door shut softly and Eleanor was alone at last with the man she loved more than her life. He removed his jacket. Apart from some suspicious dark patches on his breeches he looked remarkably unscathed. She recalled the frightful moment when Smithson had stabbed him in the back.

'Alex, has anyone seen to your back?'

'Not as yet, it was a mere scratch, I can no longer feel it.'

She scrambled out of bed her odd night-gown ballooning out around her. 'Quickly, remove your shirt and let me look. There's water in the jug, I can clean it for you.'

He grinned. 'It had been my intention to undress, my darling, but not for that purpose.'

His shirt was tossed carelessly to the floor, but not before she saw the patch of red on the back.

'Turn around, I shall clean the punctures for you.' Carefully moistening a clean linen cloth she sponged his back. 'Now the blood is removed I can see you were correct, Alex. I was worrying unnecessarily.'

Slowly he twisted to face her, a smile playing around his lips. 'My darling, I have seen you in some extraordinary garments but my nightshirt has to be the most outlandish of them all.'

'That is easily solved, my dearest.' She raised her arms.

'In which case, sweetheart, I shall remove it for you.' This was the first time she had been totally unclothed in his presence. His eyes glowed and she felt her breasts harden under his gaze.

'There's a bath in my dressing-room, I'm afraid I have used yours.'

As she spoke he was stripping off his final garments. 'With your permission, sweetheart, I shall dispense with my ablutions until the morning. I have more urgent business to attend to.'

We do hope that you have enjoyed reading this large print book.

Did you know that all of our titles are available for purchase?

We publish a wide range of high quality large print books including:
Romances, Mysteries, Classics
General Fiction
Non Fiction and Westerns

Special interest titles available in large print are:
The Little Oxford Dictionary
Music Book
Song Book
Hymn Book
Service Book

Also available from us courtesy of Oxford University Press:
Young Readers' Dictionary
(large print edition)
Young Readers' Thesaurus
(large print edition)

For further information or a free brochure, please contact us at:
Ulverscroft Large Print Books Ltd.,
The Green, Bradgate Road, Anstey,
Leicester, LE7 7FU, England.
Tel: (00 44) 0116 236 4325
Fax: (00 44) 0116 234 0205

Other titles published by
The House of Ulverscroft:

TWO GENTLEMEN FROM LONDON

Fenella-Jane Miller

When Colonel Robert Sinclair and his friend Major Simon Dudley arrive unannounced, Annabel Bentley is greatly displeased. She and her mother, Lady Sophia, have been hiding from her stepfather, Sir Randolph Rushton, for years — and Rushton is well-known to the colonel. Now it's only a matter of time before their whereabouts is revealed and Rushton arrives to snatch them back . . . unless the two gentlemen from London prove to be more than chance acquaintances . . .

THE GHOSTS OF NEDDINGFIELD HALL

Fenella-Jane Miller

When Miss Culley and her entire staff vanish without trace from Neddingfield Hall, Hester Frobisher believes she alone can solve the mystery and find her great-aunt. However, she's obliged to accept help from her cousin Ralph, the Earl of Waverley. Ralph, a formidable veteran of the Peninsular Wars, convinces Hester that they can make an invincible team. But sinister forces are at work to lure the two, and those around them, towards their deaths. No one at Neddingfield is safe. There's something seeking to destroy them. Is it ghosts? Can Hester's quick wits and Ralph's courage save them all?